A WEB OF CIRCUMSTANCES

A WEB OF CIRCUMSTANCES

Jeffrey Ashford

Chivers Press • G.K. Hall & Co.
Bath, England Thorndike, Maine USA

This Large Print edition is published by Chivers Press, England, and by G.K. Hall & Co., USA.

Published in 1999 in the U.K. by arrangement with Severn House Publishers Ltd.

Published in 1999 in the U.S. by arrangement with Chivers Press Limited.

U.K.   Hardcover   ISBN 0-7540-3545-X   (Chivers Large Print)
U.K.   Softcover   ISBN 0-7540-3546-8   (Camden Large Print)
U.S.   Softcover   ISBN 0-7838-0372–9   (Nightingale Series Edition)

The text of this Large Print edition is unabridged.
Other aspects of the book may vary from the original edition.

Set in 16 pt. New Times Roman.

Printed in Great Britain on acid-free paper.

British Library Cataloguing in Publication Data available

Library of Congress Cataloging-in-Publication Data

Ashford, Jeffrey, 1926–
        A web of circumstances / Jeffrey Ashford.
        p. (large print) cm.
        ISBN 0-7838-0372–9 (lg. print : sc : alk. paper)
        1. Large type books.   I. Title.
        [PR6060.E43W43   1997]
        823'.914—dc21   98–36970

CHAPTER ONE

As Gregg studied the chiselled features of the judge, he wondered if it really was possible for the other to expel from his mind all preconceptions, prejudices, and predilections, until the verdict was given; could any man view someone accused of as nasty a crime as rape with the total dispassion and presumption of innocence that justice demanded?

Musgrove hitched up his gown with a jerk of the shoulders, flicked one of the tails of his wig away from his neck, looked down at the opened brief on a reading-stand, faced the jury-box. 'Members of the jury, Mr Patrick Lipman is charged with that on the fourth of March . . .'

Yates rose. 'My lord, it is with the greatest regret that I interrupt my learned friend's opening address, but I deem it essential to do so since at issue is a point of law which may well go to the heart of the case.'

As far as the two QCs were concerned, Gregg thought, it was a case of back-to-front. Prosecuting counsel should be all stern rectitude, defence counsel should exude the milk of human sympathy. Yet Musgrove was short and tubby, had an engaging smile, and the many chins of a *bon viveur*, while Yates looked all Calvinistic reserve.

1

The judge said: 'I presume, Mr Yates, you have weighed your words with great care?'

'Indeed, my lord.'

He turned to the jury-box. 'You will retire so that the court can hear counsel on a matter concerned with procedure, not evidence.'

The door at the back of the jury-box was opened by an usher. When no one else moved, Gregg realised that since he had been nominated foreman, he was expected to take the lead, even though his ignorance was as great as that of the other eleven.

They followed the usher along a short corridor that smelled of dust and went into an oblong room that smelled of more dust even though superficially clean. The walls were painted in two shades of institutional brown, the linoleum's colour was not easily determined; the large table, on which were set out paper and twelve disposable ball-point pens, was uncompromisingly utilitarian; there were no curtains and the window glass was opaque; the framed list of rules and regulations had the yellowish tinge of age.

'March us in and almost immediately march us out; how stupid can they get?' The speaker was a short, slight man, in late middle age, whose words were belligerent, but whose tone had the hint of a whine to it. 'Why are they mucking us around like this?'

All eleven looked at Gregg, expecting him to be able to answer, as if he were an expert on legal procedure. The British, he thought, so often respected a title to the extent that they automatically accorded its possessor the qualities it was supposed to represent. 'All I can suggest is that counsel wants to raise a point which we musn't hear for fear we might be prejudiced by it.'

'Such as what?'

'I've no idea. Which is just as well since otherwise I might be prejudiced.' His questioner was clearly irritated rather than amused by his answer. Diana was equally critical of his sense of humour.

Another man brought a pack of cigarettes out of his coat pocket.

'It's no smoking,' said the over-large woman with the air of a bossy governess.

'Yeah? Who says?'

With open satisfaction, she pointed to a notice to the right of the doorway.

The man silently swore as he angrily thrust the pack back in his pocket.

'I hope this case isn't going to go on and on,' said a young woman with long black hair.

'It's gone on too long already,' said the man who wanted to smoke.

'I've just started in a new job and the boss didn't at all like me being called away to come here.'

'There's nothing he can do about it.'

'I know, but if I'm away too long, he ... Well, maybe find some way of replacing me.'

3

'Sue him and make a bomb.'

Gregg thought that, in theory, a citizen welcomed the chance to honour his duty to assist in the administration of justice; in practice, he felt aggrieved by the wasted time . . .

'Excuse me.'

He turned to face a man of roughly his own age who, like he, was dressed in a suit. As soon as he made eye contact, the other looked away.

'I'm Roland Sharman.'

'John Gregg.'

'I wondered if you know when we finish?'

'That's virtually impossible to judge at the moment. It depends on how many witnesses are called, how long it takes them to give their evidence, and so on.'

'I meant . . . tonight.'

'Someone told me that the court adjourns at four, but I don't know how correct that is.'

'And will we then be locked up in a hotel?'

'I hope not.' Gregg smiled. 'I'm meant to be going out to dinner. As far as I know, it's only when we're considering our verdict that we're held incommunicado.'

'I do hope you're right. Mrs Russell looks after my cats when I'm not there, but she doesn't really understand them. They're Abyssinians.'

It seemed he was expected to make some comment. 'Really?'

'They're very affectionate; sometimes, too

4

affectionate, I suppose.'

The man who had wanted to smoke was standing nearby and he chuckled. 'I reckon that's what the little lady's going to be saying.'

'What little lady?' Sharman asked.

'The one who's saying she was raped. She obviously doesn't know her Confucius. Woman with skirt up run faster than man with trouser down.'

'Hardly an appropriate remark to make,' snapped the woman who had stopped him from smoking.

'You reckon?'

'Not only is it prejudging the evidence, it's very offensive.'

'Sounds like you go for women's lib and all that caper.'

'Let's forget it,' said Gregg pleasantly, conscious that as a would-be mediator, he'd possibly annoy both parties to the argument.

*   *   *

Founded in the Middle Ages, when it had become a centre of the wool trade, Addington had grown very little until after the Second World War when it had been chosen as a development town and commercial interests had been encouraged or bribed to relocate there. Within ten years, it had virtually doubled in size and lost most of its character.

Gregg changed down into second and drove

up the steeply rising road to the very sharp bend which called for first because his Escort was suffering its years with increasing difficulty. Once round the corner—which brought him into Ifor Road—he accelerated, but not too fiercely, until the road levelled out. A hundred yards further on, he turned into the drive of Ankover Lodge.

Diana's Mercedes was in front of the garage, which surprised him since that morning she'd said she'd so much work to do at the gallery, she would be back only just in time to change before they went out. As he parked behind the Mercedes, he wondered if she'd be in as bitchy a mood as she had before he'd left that morning? There was truth in the adage that a man proposed to one woman and found he was married to another. The lucky man only made that discovery after many years. He climbed out of the Ford and didn't bother to lock it, despite the fact that locally a couple of cars had recently been stolen from drives. No self-respecting criminal would be seen in so ancient and battered a vehicle.

Althorpe was on his knees weeding one of the four lozenge-shaped flower beds in the front lawn. 'Afternoon, George,' Gregg called out.

'Is it over, then?' Althorpe asked as he put down the hand fork and looked up.

'Far from it.' Gregg came to a stop halfway along the York stone path that went from the

6

drive to the front door. 'It hasn't really started yet.'

'How's that?'

'Things didn't happen until late on, then the lawyers spent their time in arguing— thankfully, we didn't have to listen to them.'

'Sounds a daft way of doing things.'

'Much greater men than I have called the law "an ass, an idiot".' Gregg continued on his way after one of the longer conversations he had had with the usually taciturn Althorpe. He unlocked the heavy, studded wooden door and entered. The house, built in Edwardian times, had been designed by an architect who had apparently believed that wasted space was an indication of social standing and the hall was of bombastic proportions. However, Diana had furnished it with great care and the pair of carved wood and gilt girandoles, pair of harewood and inlaid side-tables, early walnut longcase clock, pair of fauteuils with original ormolu mounts, four oil-paintings by Ralph Hightowers, and carved statuary marble mantelpiece combined to add taste to overcome such perverted snobbery.

A low buzz of sound came from the television room, aka the breakfast-room. He hung his mackintosh in the small cupboard to the side of the cloakroom, crossed the hall to the third door. As he entered, Joe barked a welcome, jumped down from Diana's lap and, tail wagging, waddled up to him to be patted,

7

but Diana merely looked away from the screen for a moment, nodded, returned to her viewing. Confirmation that a bitch could be a man's best friend as well as his worst?

The credits began to roll and she switched off the set with the remote control. 'Why do they make such stupid programmes?'

'Because of the LCD factor.'

'What are you talking about?'

'Lowest common denominator.'

'Why do you keep saying ridiculous things?'

'I have a disorganised mind.' A facetious humour had become his defence against the reality of their marriage; he was surprised she had never realised that. 'I need a drink. May I get you one?'

'Have you forgotten we're off to Vera and Jim? You know what happened the last time we went to them. You and he drank so much you ended up singing embarrassingly smutty school songs.'

'It was entirely his fault for starting with Krug, continuing with Romanée-Conti, and ending with a silken cognac whose name escaped me.'

'Hardly surprising, since by then you were incapable.'

'I offer a nostalgic *mea maxima culpa* . . . However, even in the unlikely event that again such delights await, I do need an immediate reviver. Today, I've learned that hell really is other people.'

'Is that supposed to be clever?'

'Sartre probably thought so . . . Would you like something?'

'Nothing.'

He left, returned to the hall and went down a passage, halfway along which was a door lined with green baize. This marked the beginning of the servants' quarters. A relic of the past.

The kitchen had been equipped with every labour-saving device on the market and yet still looked and felt bare because of its size; beyond was an equally large pantry and a utility room. Drinks—except for wine—were kept in the pantry. He poured himself a gin and tonic, returned to the kitchen for ice. As he closed the right-hand refrigerator door, Joe entered, came to a stop, and stared beseechingly up at him. 'When a lady looks at me with such eager anticipation, I haven't the heart to deny her.' He brought down from a shelf a tin of chocolate biscuits, broke one in half, gave her a piece. She wolfed it down as if she had not been fed in days, silently begged for more. He fed her the rest and she once more begged. 'Sorry, but you've had your ration.'

When he returned to the television room, Diana was smiling at something she had read in a magazine. He sat. Diana, he thought as he drank, should smile more often. As well as her mother's midnight-black hair, deep blue eyes, pertly retroussé nose, and gentle complexion, she had inherited a mouth whose lines suggested distance, at times disdain; yet, unlike her mother, when she smiled, distance and disdain vanished.

'Joe's licking her lips,' she said.

'Bad manners.'

'You gave her something to eat in the kitchen.'

'She looked at me with such yearning trust I had to sustain her image of me.'

'And I suppose you forgot the vet said she was much too fat and out of condition and if she doesn't lose weight, her heart will be damaged?'

'I remembered, which is why I gave her so little biscuit that she hardly had time to taste it before it was gone.'

'You gave her just as much as she could eat, didn't you?'

'Why would I go and do that?'

'Because you want her to die.'

'Come off it . . . What's gone wrong? What's happened to upset you?'

He was surprised to note how disturbed his questions had obviously made her.

'Nothing's happened,' she snapped.

'Sure?'

'I've just said so, haven't I? Why d'you go on and on?'

'Because I think there's been some sort of trouble. For one thing, this morning you said you'd be back so late it would be a terrible rush

10

to change and get to Vera and Jim in time, yet you were back before me.'

'Things were easier than I thought.'

'It seems a bit of a contradiction . . .'

'I've a thumping head.' She stood. 'I'm going to lie down until it's time to go.'

He watched her leave, followed by Joe.

CHAPTER TWO

The quality and quantity of the wines and liqueurs had matched Gregg's hopes and he was happy to settle back in the front passenger seat of the Mercedes and contemplate a world that was painted in soft, sweet colours.

They rounded a bend and the headlights picked out a stop sign. As the car came to a halt, she said: 'I made a point of telling Frank you write.'

'Oh!'

'Is that all you can say?'

'For the moment, yes.'

'He's a very nice man.'

'He certainly has prosperous manners.'

'He's a senior partner in one of the big City financial firms.'

'Of course!'

She turned right. 'Why do you sneer at anyone who's successful?'

'Naked jealousy.'

'That's really stupid.'

'I must be allowed to excel at something.'

'My God, I sometimes wonder why I bother ... When he heard you write, he said how he envied you.'

'An envy guaranteed to disappear at the doors of his bank.'

'Why are you going on being ridiculous?'

'In vino, very ass.'

'Can you be infuriating!' She slowed for crossroads. 'He asked me if you do any work for television; said a great friend of his is very high up in one of the TV companies.'

They reached a two-mile straight and since it was free of traffic, she increased speed a long way above the legal limit. He was unperturbed, insulated by alcohol and faith in the skill of her driving.

'I told him how you'd always wanted to work for TV, but didn't have the right contacts to get anyone interested in your work. He promised to introduce you to his friend. Isn't that good?'

'Indeed.'

'You hardly sound enthusiastic.'

It would hardly be diplomatic to explain his embarrassment at the thought of her so clearly touting on his behalf. 'By tomorrow morning, he'll have forgotten every word of the conversation.'

'Why are you such a pessimist?'

'My maternal grandmother was Swedish.'

'I suppose the real truth is, you don't like my helping you because you think it's an implied criticism of you.'

'I'll answer when I've worked that out.'

'You hate being reminded that I have to pay almost all the upkeep of the house.'

'Do you remember how, before you bought Ankover, I suggested we went on looking for somewhere smaller and very much cheaper?'

'And do you remember I said I wasn't going to slum?'

Shortly before their marriage, he'd been offered a well-built, attractive bungalow, pleasantly situated, surrounded by a generous garden, at a price which he could just, optimistically, afford with the help of a mortgage. Since love had still been blind, he'd failed to realise that her refusal to consider such a home had been motivated not by practical reasons, but snobbery . . .

They passed through south Addington, an area of old terrace houses and new estates, to reach the station and Bank Street—home of thirty-nine of the forty thieves—which brought them to High Street and North Street, a name that always amused him since it ran virtually due east. Halfway along North Street, they turned left into Adeane Road which became Ifor Road beyond the sharp bend, for a reason lost in the mists of time, halfway up the steep hill.

She braked to a halt just short of the

entrance to the drive of Ankover Lodge. He unclipped the seat-belt, stepped out on to the pavement. Walking with considerable concentration, he went up the drive to his Ford. He started the engine and engaged reverse, but let the clutch out too sharply and stalled. His second attempt was more successful and he backed onto the road so that she could drive into the garage—single, because when the house had been built, no one had envisaged the two-car family. As he waited, he hoped that no patrolling police would arrive and wonder if he were in a fit state to be in charge of a car.

The Mercedes entered the garage and he drove back in. He followed her along the stone path to the front door and there searched his pockets for the key.

'In your right-hand trouser pocket,' she said, with strained patience.

'I've looked there.'

'Look again.'

The key had been caught up in his handkerchief. As she preceded him inside, he wondered why women were so often right about the small things in life, but wrong about the large ones? He began to walk towards the stairs.

'What about the alarm?'

He hurriedly turned round and crossed to the cloakroom in which was the control panel. If the right combination were not fed in within

14

sixty seconds of the door's having been opened . . . Was the number 431469 or 341469 . . . ?

She pushed past him and punched in the six figures. 'Mother's always said that a man in his cups is more useless than a broken whisk.'

Her mother said many things about men, none flattering.

He followed her across to the graceful, curving staircase, with elaborate wrought-iron balustrade. As they climbed the stairs, he tried to prepare himself for further complaints. They went down the right-hand passage to their bedroom suite. The bedroom was large enough not to be overburdened by the majestic four-poster bed which she had rescued from a house in North Wales and had had restored by craftsmen so skilful that only the most detailed examination would reveal their work.

She came to a stop in the centre of the room. 'Would you like to help me out of my frock?'

It was a signal, whose origins went back to their honeymoon, that she would welcome sex, but it was so long since she had last employed it, and her mood until then had seemed so unresponsive, that he was surprised and did not immediately respond.

'Don't tell me that wine really doth undoeth man?' she said as she came forward.

*   *   *

She fell asleep almost as soon as the lights were switched off and was soon making quick, muted noises at the back of her throat, like a puppy's distant whimpers. He wondered what had so unexpectedly aroused her passion? If only he could identify the cause, how much warmer the future might be . . .

The telephone rang, startling him. Because a call at this time of night automatically created tension, he reached for the phone with clumsy haste and knocked a book onto the floor.

'What . . . what . . .' she mumbled.

He switched on the bedside light, picked up the receiver. 'Yes?'

'Listen and listen good. You're the foreman, so if you want to stay healthy, see he's not found guilty. And keep away from the cops or you're history.' The line went dead.

He slowly lowered the receiver.

'Who was it?' she asked thickly. She sat up and the sheet and single blanket fell away to reveal her shapely breasts. 'Was it Mother? Has she been taken ill; has she had an accident?'

'Nothing to do with her.'

'Then who was it? What do they want?'

He automatically shielded her from the unease the call had engendered. 'Damned if I know. Sounded like someone was tight and he dialled the wrong number.'

'Bloody man!' She lay back and pulled up

16

the bedclothes. 'It'll take me hours to get back to sleep.'

He switched off the light. It was going to take him longer to sleep than it would her. The call confused as much as worried him. A joke? Could it have been the juror, Hendry? Hendry was so egregiously bumptious and insensitive that he would think it a joke to make such a call. Yet the speaker's voice had been totally different from his and even allowing for the effect of distortion over the line, it seemed very difficult to accept it had been he. And had it been, in all probability he would have stayed on the line to discover how his 'joke' was received. Yet the alternative to a joke was that the threat was genuine. In the recent past, there had been reported a couple of incidents in which threats had been made to jury members to try to make them deliver false verdicts . . . In the morning, he would report what had happened to the police; they could decide how genuine was the call.

CHAPTER THREE

For years the Addington police had repeatedly been promised a new divisional HQ. Promises were cheap. They still had to work from several small buildings, mostly old, often unsuitable, grouped around a square which

17

offered space for fewer cars than needed to park there.

The public entrance was in the middle of the largest building. Gregg opened the right-hand swing door and stepped into the front room. There was a counter, behind which stood a PC who was talking to an elderly lady, two noticeboards on the far wall on which were pinned a forest of papers, a round table on which were several magazines which looked as if they'd been there a long time, and four chairs that had seen better days; only radio equipment in the communications room beyond the counter, partially visible through the open doorway, suggested C Division had moved with the times.

The PC nodded at Gregg, continued to speak to the woman. She became annoyed and her voice rose; a uniformed sergeant came out of the communications room, spoke briefly to the PC, then to her. The PC moved down the counter. 'How can I help you?'

'My name's Gregg and something's happened ... I'm on the jury in the Lipman case that's being heard at Shinstone and last night I received a telephone call at home threatening me that if I don't make certain he's not found guilty, I'll be in trouble.'

The PC's expression had sharpened. 'Right, Mr Gregg. You'll need a word with CID. Perhaps you'll hang on whilst I get hold of someone? Why not sit down over there?'

Gregg crossed to one of the chairs set around the table. He picked up a magazine and leafed through it, came to a stop at an article on Barbados . . . The previous winter, Diana had wanted him to go to Barbados for a long holiday. He'd refused to do so on the grounds that he could afford neither the time nor the cost. His refusal had angered her. She'd pay for both of them and if he didn't finish his book for another couple of months, were there going to be riots outside the bookshops? She simply could not understand his need to maintain his pride. But then wealth inevitably blunted a person's sympathies . . .

A tall, well-built man, in his middle twenties, came up to where he sat. 'Mr Gregg? I'm Detective Constable Menzies. Would you come this way so we can have a chat?'

He followed Menzies across the front room to the second of two doors, then along a corridor and into an interview room. He sat on one side of the oblong table on which were a recording unit, an ashtray, some loose paper, and a couple of ballpoint pens. Menzies put a notebook down on the table, opened this, picked up one of the pens. 'We'd better sort out the preliminaries. If I can have your full name and address?'

He gave these.

'Now, if you'd like to tell me what happened.'

He did so.

19

Menzies finished writing, looked up. 'Those are the exact words he used?'

'As near as I can remember them.'

'He didn't mention Lipman's name?'

'No.'

'You said the call startled you which means your mind could have been a bit haywire, so how certain can you be?'

'Perfectly certain.'

Menzies smiled briefly. 'Sorry if I keep on and on asking the same question, but it is important and I need to be sure... You wondered whether it could be another juryman. Why did you?'

'One of them is the kind of person who could easily think it funny to make that sort of a call.'

'On reflection, d'you think it could have been him?'

'Very unlikely. The voice was completely different; it was harshly pitched and rough.'

'Uneducated?'

'If one's allowed to say that these days, yes.'

'What's the name of the man who you first thought might possibly have made the call?'

Gregg hesitated. 'Will you question him to make certain it wasn't he?'

'Probably.'

'I wouldn't like him to think I actually accused him. I mean... Well, it's not a pleasant thing to do.'

'We'll not name you unless it becomes

necessary.'

In the detective's eyes, Gregg wondered, was he informer or law-abiding citizen?

'Sidney Hendry.'

'When you were at the courthouse, did anyone who wasn't an official or on the jury try to make contact with you?'

'No. At least, I wasn't conscious of anyone's having done so.'

'Has anything unusual happened that could be connected with this threat?'

'In what way?'

'Sometimes, a bit of pressure is put on. Could be as simple as forcing a lock and making that obvious; just something to make you think that if they can do that, they can probably do much worse.'

'There's been nothing like that.'

Menzies stared down at his notebook for a moment, then looked up. 'One last question. Why have you reported this?'

Gregg's voice expressed his surprise. 'If this is a genuine attempt to suborn me, it's my duty to report it.'

'Yeah. Of course.' Menzies closed his notebook. 'That's it, then.' He led the way back to the front room, shook hands. 'Thanks for coming along.'

*   *   *

Detective Sergeant Park had begun to discover

21

the torments of age; his hair was thinning at the crown, his waistline had expanded more than he was ready to admit, energetic exercise caused him quickly to become short of breath, and attractive young women dismissed him as scenery—although contentedly married, it would have been nice to have been accorded some interest.

He was well aware that the younger members of the force often referred to him as Uncle Tom, but he believed this nickname to be no more than amused recognition of his old-fashioned attitudes and, to their prejudiced eyes, totally out-of-date ideas. And if some of his seniors considered him lucky to have made sergeant, that was because they had forgotten that dependability was often more valuable than thrusting imagination.

He was saddened by the evidence of man's endless capacity for evil, but sufficient of an optimist to remember that beyond his work lay a world in which most people tried to lead good lives; evil might appear to have all the good tunes, but a good listener could always hear the angels clearing their throats before they began to sing louder.

He looked across the desk at Menzies. 'Do we know what this Lipman is charged with?'

'I checked and it's rape; date rape, really. He says she was all for it, she says she tried to make him stop.'

'What's Lipman's background?'

'For the past three years, he's worked for the Pemberton Security Company—that's a small local outfit. They give him a good reference.'

'Any form?'

'None on the books and none that's been wiped.'

'Have you checked him out in the Yellow Book?' Park asked, referring to the list of named suspects who had never been brought to trial because of lack of proof.

'He's not listed.'

'Then he seems to be as clean as a whistle?'

'That's the size of things.'

Park brushed the palm of his hand over his head, subconsciously trying to smooth his hair to conceal his growing baldness. 'It doesn't sound like anyone could be sufficiently interested in him to try to fix a jury. So what about Gregg?'

'Middle or late thirties; well spoken, obviously educated; lives in Ifor Road which means he doesn't have to scratch around for the odd fiver.'

'Not the type to try to have fun at our expense?'

'Good, honest citizen from head to toe. Even solemnly said he reported the call because it was his duty to do so!'

'You find that odd?'

'Sarge, this is the end of the century, not the beginning.'

23

'More's the pity.'

Menzies smiled.

'So you reckon he's genuine?'

'Sure of it.' He added, in an affected accent: 'It's not done, old man, to try to take the mickey out of our noble boys in blue.'

'Highly humorous . . . So we're back to the question, who's going to take the risk of trying to fix this jury? Could it be someone's idea of a joke after all?'

'Like I said, Gregg did suggest the possibility, but he wasn't really batting for it.'

'Yet he named a possible joker?'

Menzies brought out his notebook, flicked through the pages until he found the one he wanted. 'Sidney Hendry.'

'Question him. And have a word with whoever runs the security firm and find out what sort of scale they work to. If it's really high, maybe someone's turned Lipman and he was due to feed 'em information of a really big job, but if he's found guilty and jailed, he won't be able to.'

'That's a point, skipper,' Menzies said, not quite hiding his surprise at Park's imaginative suggestion.

*   *   *

When Gregg turned into the drive, Diane was in the front garden, selecting and cutting long-stemmed rosebuds—flower arranging, at which

24

she was gifted, was a favourite occupation of hers. As he crossed the lawn, she carefully laid down a stem in the trug, then straightened up.

'Were there any limes?'

'Damn!'

'Don't say you forgot.'

'Then I'll remain silent.'

'You are hopeless.'

'I'll make amends by nipping back to see if I can find some.'

'I must have them because I want to try out the new pudding on us before I give it to Carol and Henry.'

'Does that mean they're coming here?'

'Don't you ever listen to what I say? I told you when I asked you to get the limes that Carol had phoned and I'd invited them for dinner on Tuesday.'

She had not mentioned their coming, but he saw no point in contradicting her. There would be argument, sulking, resentment . . .

'Why don't you like her?' she asked, then bent down and picked up the trug.

'I don't dislike her. I just view her with great care.'

'I suppose that's because she told you she got one of your books out of the library and found it difficult.'

'Her lack of reading ability calls for sympathy, not judgment. I view her carefully because she's conditioned by her jealousy of you. Her smiles and her compliments are etched with acid.'

'I suppose she is jealous of me,' she said complacently. 'After all, Henry's never been a success and made much money.'

'Despite which, he hasn't led a very happy life.'

'You say the most ridiculous things.'

'That is one of my more attractive qualities . . . Remind me how many limes you want?'

'They're very expensive, so just a kilo.'

'I will ask for two and a fifth pounds to show my opinion of European standards.'

'I'm not going to do any more gardening— it's beginning to get my back.'

'Then let me carry the clobber.' He took the trug from her.

'Have you looked at the runner beans?' she asked.

'Not recently.'

'I told George to pick some yesterday for lunch and he said they weren't ready. Why do his sort always want to leave vegetables to grow until they become coarse?'

'Their logic is simple. The larger something becomes, the more one gets for one's money.'

'It's my money, not his.'

'Metaphorically speaking. Anyway, he'll view everything he grows as if it were his own produce.'

'Are you saying he pinches things?'

'Good God, no! All I'm suggesting is he views the stuff here in the same light as the

26

vegetables he grows for himself at home.'
Privately, he thought it probable Althorpe
quietly did take some of the produce; after all,
that was a perk which employed gardeners had
enjoyed throughout the ages. But she would
never accept that fact with equanimity. Like
most wealthy people, she guarded even her
most insignificant possessions with bitter
determination.

As they walked across the lawn, he decided
not to tell her about his visit to the police
station. In her present mood, she'd delight in
pointing out that he'd obviously lied to her the
previous night when he'd said he didn't know
what to make of the telephone call.

CHAPTER FOUR

Hendry lived in a semi-detached in Spursham,
a town ten miles to the north of Addington
which was small enough to have escaped the
onslaught of chain stores and so still enjoyed a
number of independently run shops, the most
notable of which was a bakery which produced
crisp, crunchy bread.

He had married a woman of little
intelligence, but great forbearance; she even
managed to laugh at his jokes. He had two
teenage children who treated him with
contempt, but saw this as a reflection of their

generation, not of himself.

'Are you're sure you're a detective?' he asked, as he stood in the front doorway. 'I mean, where's the deerstalker and meerschaum pipe?'

Oh my God! Menzies thought.

'So what's the problem? Have I been caught parking on a solid line?'

'I expect so.'

'I ask for mercy on the grounds that I'm a poor orphan, having murdered my parents last week.'

'I'm here on an important matter, Mr Hendry, so if we could have a talk?'

'Come in, dear sir; enter my humble abode.'

As Menzies stepped into the hall, which was festooned with knick-knacks, a woman looked out from the end room.

'My better half! Come forward, Daphne, and meet the great Holmes's successor. Everything you say will be taken down in evidence and used against you, so admit to nothing other than conspiring to blow up parliament for the good of the country.'

'Good afternoon,' she said nervously.

'Good afternoon, Mrs Hendry. Sorry to break in on you on a Saturday afternoon, but I need to ask your husband a few questions.'

'Is . . . is something wrong?'

He smiled reassuringly. 'Nothing to cause any concern here.' He turned to Hendry. 'So if we could go somewhere?'

28

'Come into my parlour said the fly to the spider.' Hendry flung open the door of the front room. 'My dear, our visitor would like some tea or coffee . . .'

'Nothing for me, thanks,' Menzies cut in.

'I forgot. No drinking on duty . . . Enter!'

Menzies went into the room, his sympathy for the wife increasing with every moment.

'Sit down. No extra charge for parking one's bottom in this area.'

He sat. 'I understand you're on the jury in the Lipman trial?'

'I am indeed one of the twelve good men and true, sworn to judge the facts. And if you ask me . . .'

'I'm not.'

'All I was going to say was . . .'

'Weren't you advised not to discuss the case with anyone?'

'But you're a policeman.'

'Makes no difference.'

'If you're not going to talk about it, why are you here?'

'To ask if you made a telephone call late last night or in the early hours of the morning?'

'Not me.'

'You didn't make a call to someone concerning the trial?'

Hendry hesitated. 'No.'

'Are you quite certain?'

'Well . . . Tell the truth and shame the devil. I did get on to Eric and have a bit of a chat.

29

But only to tell him the case was about rape so maybe there'd be some, you know, interesting details . . .' He became silent as he saw the look of contempt on Menzies's face.

'Did you phone anyone else?'

'No.'

'You did not make a call to Mr Gregg?'

'Who's he? Don't know anyone by that name.'

'He is the foreman of the jury.'

'Oh, him! Yeah, I'd forgotten. Bit of a starchy upmarket, if you know what I mean.'

'Someone phoned him and threatened him if he did not ensure a certain verdict was reached. That is a very serious offence.'

'I'm sure it is. But what makes you think I could ever do a thing like that?'

'Perhaps you might regard it as a joke?'

'I like a good joke as much as the next man, but that doesn't mean I'll go about the place threatening anyone. No way. You've just got to believe me.'

'Have I?'

Small beads of perspiration had begun to dot Hendry's forehead. 'You can't really think it could've been me.'

'You might not have realised it was a criminal offence.'

'I couldn't do it. Do I look like a bloke who'd threaten someone?'

He looked like a punctured balloon.

The silence goaded Hendry into rushing

30

across to the doorway and shouting: 'Daphne, Daphne, come here quickly.' He turned back. 'She'll tell you.'

Daphne, worried, uncertain, hurried into the room.

'He thinks I've been threatening people; ringing 'em up and being nasty. Tell him I couldn't do such a thing. Go on, tell him.'

She was bewildered.

'Mrs Hendry,' Menzies said quietly, 'when did you both go to bed last night?'

'Well . . . I mean . . . I didn't really notice.'

'Just roughly will do.'

'I suppose it was soon after eleven. I mean, that's when we usually go.'

'Would you say you both fell asleep quickly?'

'He did. Always does.' There was a touch of resentment in her voice. 'But it always takes me a long time and then I don't sleep well; haven't done since I had the last one.'

'Have you any idea when you did fall asleep?'

She shook her head.

'Did you husband remain asleep all the time you were awake?'

She nodded.

'Do you have a telephone extension in your bedroom?'

'No.'

'Tell him I'd never threaten anyone,' Hendry demanded.

31

'He couldn't,' she said weakly.

Menzies silently agreed.

*　　*　　*

The Rune ran through the centre of Shinstone and for no particular reason other than history, the smart part of town, both commercial and residential, was to the south of the river; the offices of Pemberton Security lay well to the north. Menzies entered the ugly red-brick, building and, following the signs, climbed one flight of stairs and crossed to a door with frosted glass on which was the firm's name. Inside, he introduced himself to the woman who worked at a desk and asked to speak to whoever was in charge. She left, to reappear and then lead the way along a short corridor and into a room whose furnishings were as utilitarian as those of the reception area. Ryan, a large, thickly built man, with a face that looked unfinished, came round the desk, shook hands, and in a few sentences let it be known that when he'd been in the county force, he'd been a superintendent. Menzies was unimpressed.

Ryan settled behind the desk. 'So what's this about?'

'I'm hoping you can give me some gen on Lipman.'

'Bit late in the day for that, surely?'

Menzies ignored the comment. 'How did

32

you find him as an employee?'

'I've already told you lot . . . Reliable, hard working, capable of showing some initiative.'

'Any problems with the ladies?'

'Here in the office? No.'

'D'you know anything about his lifestyle?'

'Why are you asking?'

'Just the usual general interest.'

'Balls! You're after something else. What is it?'

Menzies decided there was no point in continuing to deny the truth. 'One of the jury at Lipman's trial claims he's been threatened and told to ensure there's not a guilty verdict.'

'Has he, by God!'

'So we're wondering whether the threat's a joke or for real.'

'And?'

'If it's for real, then there's someone out there who's very eager for Lipman to stay free. Why? Maybe because if he's at work, he can make it easy for a big job to be pulled.'

Ryan opened the top right-hand drawer of his desk and brought out a pack of cigarettes. 'D'you use these?'

'No, thanks.'

He tapped out a cigarette, lit it. 'You can forget that possibility. We're a small firm, doing our best to stay alive in the face of the big bastards who are always trying to get bigger at our expense. We've made a name for ourselves for reliability and there's no one can

33

foul-mouth us, but if someone wants to move a million, he inevitably reckons to go for size because he thinks it safer. We never handle a job big enough to make it worthwhile taking the risk and expense of trying to keep Lipman out of jail by fixing the jury.'

'You've no known big jobs coming up in the future?'

'That's what I've said,' snapped Ryan.

Rank never forgot itself, Menzies thought. 'Like I asked earlier, d'you know anything about his lifestyle?'

'I'd be a poor security boss if I didn't keep both eyes wide open for heavy spending. Lipman lives in a cheap flat on the outskirts of Frencham, drives a four-year-old car, dresses badly like everyone else, and his last holiday was package at the cheap end of the market.'

'Thanks for your help.' Menzies stood.

Ryan, not bothering to get to his feet, looked up. 'My advice is to grab the bloke who says he was threatened and charge him with wasting the police's time.'

*   *   *

That Detective Inspector Noyes had the sleek, smooth appearance of a PR executive was ironic since a heady mixture of ambition and dedication to his job frequently resulted in his being anything but diplomatic. 'So Ryan's running a security firm—he'll be good at that.'

34

Park couldn't judge whether that was genuine praise or snide comment.

'Accept his evidence and no one's trying to spring Lipman because information he can give is essential to a future heist. And since he's not rich or famous, we can forget any other motive. So either it was a joke or Gregg's lying. What does Jim say about Hendry?'

Noyes often used Christian names, deeming this helpful in cementing the spirit of camaraderie so important to any specialised unit; however, he did not expect to be called by his Christian name.

'Jim puts the possibility that Hendry made the call at nil.'

'Then do we say Gregg, for some unknown reason, is lying?'

'It seems unlikely.'

'Why?'

'He lives in Ifor Road, which means he's seriously rich.'

'The rich don't lie? How the hell d'you think they became rich? . . . What about the rest of the jury—have they all been questioned to find out if any of 'em has been threatened?'

'I've had Ron and Mike checking and they say no one has.'

Noyes clasped his hands behind his head. 'Why would a rich man lie about this? What can he gain? Impossible to answer. But if he's telling the truth, who out there gives a shit whether or not Lipman's put inside? . . . We're missing out on something. What?'

Park did not try to answer.

'We're just going to have to play this as we see it now. So get through to the court and tell 'em a juror's reported that he's been threatened.'

*   *   *

The judge's reputation named him tough, but fair. He viewed crime as one of the greatest dangers to any civilisation because it poisoned from within and therefore when uncovered needed to be extirpated with the utmost rigour. Yet he would always accept that there could be mitigating factors which would lessen the degree of guilt.

'Members of the jury,' he said, his speech clipped, 'it has been brought to my attention that one of you has received a threatening telephone call designed to persuade you to bring in a specific verdict.' There was a brief hum of surprise from the public gallery, quickly checked. The reporters on the press bench wrote rapidly. Once silence had returned, the judge continued.

'Such a blatant attempt to interfere in the course of justice will not be tolerated and every possible effort is being made to identify those responsible. It is to be hoped that what I am saying now will prevent any further incident, but should any of you receive a threat, in any

36

shape or form, it will be your duty to inform the police immediately.'

*   *   *

Musgrove's opening speech introduced the facts that were to be presented in a sequence that made it obvious how each was linked to what had gone before and he explained the law on rape, with particular reference to the question of consent, both explicit and implied.

*   *   *

The doctor was called in the late afternoon. In his evidence-in-chief, he testified that he had examined the victim in the special unit at the police station and had found evidence of bruising on one arm and around the genitalia; there had been no signs of injury to her throat.

Yates rose. He hitched up his silk gown, rubbed the side of his chin with his forefinger, cleared his throat twice; mannerisms that almost always preceded his cross-examination. 'Doctor, your evidence has been clearly and, if you will allow me to say so, fairly given.' He was adept at using compliments to ease a witness off guard. 'However, there are one or two points which need further elucidation. You describe the bruising on Miss Benson's arm as readily visible, but not extensive; would you agree that it would be correct to say it was not

37

serious?'

'That is so.' The doctor spoke briskly; a busy man who hoped he would not be detained for long.

'The kind of bruising any one of us might suffer if we inadvertently banged into something?'

'Provided you did so with a measure of force.'

'And there was nothing about this bruising to suggest it must have been caused by a person rather than an object?'

'Quite impossible to identify what had caused it.'

'Were you able to judge how long before your examination this bruising was caused?'

'I could do no more than form an opinion because bruising is subject to so many variables. It develops more easily in soft, lax tissue, but a person can, deliberately or otherwise, harden his flesh until it does not bruise easily; young and old bruise more readily than someone in his prime; diet and disease affect it. Bruising is a result of blood escaping into tissues from areas that have been crushed and it changes in colour from crimson to brown, to a greenish yellow, to a pale straw colour. But it is recognised that colour is a poor guide to time elapsed. Having all those facts in mind, it was my opinion that the bruising on Miss Benson's arm was between eight and twelve hours old.'

'Was the bruising to her private parts of a similar age?'

'In so far as I could judge, yes.'

'Was this bruising of a severe nature?'

The doctor thought for a moment. 'That is a difficult question to answer.'

'I should have thought it simple enough.'

'Had the bruising been to another part of the body, it could not have been described as serious. But this region of the body is where relatively little force can cause physical injury to which, of course, must be added the considerable psychological hurt.'

Yates put his hands in the pockets of his trousers, rocked back on his heels. 'Correct me if I am wrong, Doctor, but surely there can be no psychological hurt if the patient has welcomed the physical act which caused the bruising? Or, to put it in another way, you are assuming, are you not, that in this case, the patient did not welcome the advances of Mr Lipman?'

The doctor was too experienced to be caught by so obvious a trap. 'You asked me why the question was a difficult one to answer; I have tried to explain. I am assuming nothing unless I have every reason to do so.

'We need to become more specific. Was this bruising sufficient to suggest to you that Miss Benson had been subjected to a severe physical sexual assault?'

'No.'

39

'Would you like to go further? Was it, in fact, of a relatively minor nature?'

'I would use the term, moderate.'

'Very well. I imagine you would agree that sexual intercourse between consenting adults can, according to the wishes of those participating, range from the most delicate to the most boisterous behaviour?'

'Yes.'

'And if the behaviour is boisterous, it may very well inadvertently result in bruising to the woman's private parts?'

'Yes.'

'So the bruising we are discussing may indicate no more than that the love-making was of a boisterous nature?'

'If judged in isolation, that is so.'

'It is not in your remit to judge it in any other fashion. Did you examine Miss Benson's neck?'

'Yes.'

'For what reason?'

'To determine whether there were any signs of injury.'

'Were you informed about what kind of injury you might find?'

'I was told there might be one or more cuts.'

'As from a knife?'

'That was not said.'

'But you must surely have envisaged a knife? And if you believed one had been held to Miss Benson's neck, you must have considered it far more likely that she had been raped?'

'No.'

'No? You are asking the jury to believe that when you learned that a knife had possibly been held to Miss Benson's neck, you did not believe rape to have been very much more likely?'

'It was not my job to speculate.'

'You are to be congratulated, Doctor, on your ability to forgo a speculation that nine hundred and ninety-nine other men would be unable to resist.' Yates sat.

Bastard, said the doctor silently.

Musgrove stood. 'Doctor, are you of the opinion that had Miss Benson willingly engaged in sexual intercourse, she would have suffered the bruising she did?'

'It is unlikely, but not impossible.'

'Thank you.'

*   *   *

The PC stood in the witness box as if on guard at Buckingham Palace; his answers were given staccato style. 'The call was received at 0908 hours. I logged it and then . . .'

'One moment,' cut in Musgrove. 'Who was the call from and what was its nature?'

'Mrs Benson reported that her daughter had been raped the previous night and named the man concerned.'

'What did you do?'

'Informed CID, sir.'

'Thank you, Constable.'

*   *   *

Detective Constable Anderson looked as if he thought it a long time since life had been generous to him. 'I drove to Arlington Crescent and there spoke to Mr and Mrs Benson and Miss Benson. As a result of what I was told, I requested the presence of a WPC— that is, a woman police constable.'

'Will you describe, in layman's terms, in what condition you judged Miss Benson to be?' Musgrove asked.

'She was very distressed. It was only after WPC Sloane had arrived and spoken to her that we were able to persuade her to attend the special rape unit.'

'Did you ask why she had not reported the incident at an earlier time?'

'Yes, sir. She didn't seem to be able to answer, but her mother said . . .'

'What Mrs Benson said, she herself will tell us. Miss Benson gave you no explanation?'

'None that really made sense.'

'Did you accompany her to the police station?'

'No, sir. WPC Sloane went with her. After they'd left, I asked Mrs Benson if she would give me the clothing that her daughter had been wearing when she returned home early

42

that morning.'

'Will you tell the court if the clothing which the usher will hand you—exhibits nine to fourteen—are the clothes you were given?'

Several items, each in a plastic bag, were in turn handed to the DC. He examined the identification details which bore his signatures. 'These are what Mrs Benson gave me.'

'In what state were the various items?'

'With the exception of the pair of pants, they were undamaged and unmarked, but crumpled.'

'And the pants?'

'They had been torn.'

'Will you describe the nature of the tear.'

'It extends from one leg hole to the other.'

'So that in this condition there would be no material hindrance to an act of sexual intercourse?'

'Would you prefer to give the evidence yourself?' Yates, not bothering to stand, asked with simulated indignation.

'Thank you.' Musgrove sat.

'No questions,' said Yates.

The judge looked at the electric clock above the plaque commemorating the opening of the courtroom in the thirties by the then Lord Chief Justice. 'This will be a convenient time to adjourn.' He turned to the jury. 'You will bear in mind what I said to you this morning. Should any of you receive a communication from someone unknown to you which is

43

relevant to this trial, whether or not it contains a specific threat, you are to inform the police immediately.' He stood.

The court rose.

CHAPTER FIVE

The phone rang while Diana and Gregg were watching television.

'That will be for you,' she said.

As he stood, he thought good-humouredly that if the television programme was interesting, a call always was held to be for him. He went through to the hall and picked up the receiver.

'Weren't you told to stay away from the police? Keep your mouth quiet and see it's not guilty or you'll suffer.' The line went dead.

This time, he could not keep fear at bay by wondering if the call was meant to be a joke. He dialled 999. When the operator asked him which emergency service he wanted, he said the police; as soon as the connection was made, he began to explain what had happened so hurriedly and excitedly that he hardly made sense. The woman to whom he was speaking calmed him down with professional skill, then advised him that he should report the matter to his local CID as it would be they who would handle the matter.

He checked the number of divisional HQ, dialled it. Once through, he spoke to DC Duggan who expressed neither surprise nor, indeed, any emotion. Would he, Duggan asked, be at home for the rest of the evening? Then someone would be along to have a word with him.

He replaced the receiver, conscious that the immediate sense of panic was gone. Not because the circumstances had changed, but because he had transferred the responsibility for deciding how to react. A sign of moral weakness?

He returned to the television room to find the programme had finished; Diana put down the *Radio Times* and said: 'There's nothing more.' She switched off the set without bothering to find out if there were anything he might want to watch. 'Who was that phoned?'

He sat.

'Well?' she said impatiently. Joe yapped twice, perhaps thinking her tone of voice suggested something interesting was about to happen.

'Do you remember the phone call on Friday after we'd gone to bed?'

'What's that got to do with anything?'

'It was to try to make me vote not guilty at the trial.'

'You told me you didn't know what the call was about.'

'I wasn't certain whether it was a joke and

45

didn't want to alarm you if it was.'

'Why should it have alarmed me?'

'He threatened me if I didn't do as he said. And if I wanted to stay healthy, I mustn't tell the police.'

'Then don't.'

'I reported to them what had happened on Saturday morning,' he said quietly.

'You did what? After you'd been warned? How could you be such a bloody fool?'

'If someone was trying to rig the verdict, I had to report that.'

'What's it matter to you?'

'The same as it does to anyone and everyone. If justice becomes twisted . . .'

'Not one of your sermons now. You're not wearing a dog-collar. Are you trying to be the conscience of the world?'

'I hope not . . . A detective will be along here any moment to talk about the latest call.'

'What latest one?'

'Just now.'

'That was another threat?'

'Yes.'

'Christ! Anything could happen to me now.'

'I'm the one being threatened.'

'I won't be able to sleep. I can't take any more.' She came to her feet and hurried out of the room.

Joe, on the settee, looked with goggling eyes at the door and then at him. 'Just a slight divergence of ideas and ideals,' he said. 'So

46

what's your opinion? Should one honour one's duty to the state, or should one guard one's own skin?' She jumped down onto the floor, waddled across the room and out through the open doorway. 'From a common-sense point of view, you probably have to be right.'

Time passed, then the front-door bell rang. He opened the door to face two men he had not met before who introduced themselves. Detective Inspector Noyes looked sharp and thrusting, Detective Constable Duggan, eminently forgettable. He led the way into the drawing room, very large, carefully furnished with choice pieces, touched with a certain coldness. He offered them a drink and they refused. As soon as they were seated, Noyes said briskly: 'Tell me about this call you received.'

'It was very short. The man reminded me I'd been told not to inform the police the previous time, and said if I didn't keep my mouth quiet, I'd suffer.'

'That's all?'

'I'd call it more than enough.'

'He used the actual words, "keep your mouth quiet"?'

'That's right.'

'It's an odd expression.'

'I suppose he used it because he was a foreigner.'

'What makes you say that?'

'His voice was accented—not heavily, but

47

enough to be reasonably certain he wasn't English.'

'So what nationality do you think he was?'

'Hard to judge. German maybe. The tone was guttural.'

'You didn't mention the speaker was a foreigner the previous time you reported a threat.'

'He wasn't the same man this time. The first one was definitely English.'

'So if this is meant to be a joke, there are at least two in on it?'

'It's no joke.'

'What now makes you so certain?'

'The way this second man spoke. He sounded . . . Well, truly vicious—for him, the end will always justify the means.'

'You have an expressive way of describing things. But then, of course, you are a writer.'

Gregg said quietly, but with some edge: 'Is that a roundabout way of suggesting I'm making it all up?'

'If you can write books you are an intelligent man and I'm sure you wouldn't be so stupid as to waste our time. What do you make of the threat?'

'What do you expect me to make of it beyond the obvious?'

'Have you considered what "suffer" might encompass?'

'Of course.'

'So how do you feel?'

48

'If you're asking if I'm scared, yes, I am, not least because the indefinite is usually much more alarming than the definite, thanks to imagination.'

'The threat scares you, yet you've reported it even though specifically warned not to.' Noyes's voice rose to turn the sentence into a question.

'I didn't see I had any option.'

'Why not?'

'It was my duty to report it.'

'You obviously take your moral duties very seriously.'

'Is that so unusual?'

'In this day and age, I'm afraid it is . . . Although you've told us that you've been scared, I'm sure you'll have appreciated that a threat demanding something is done can only be effective all the time the threat is not carried out. So whoever's behind this may well try to put more pressure on you, but he will not physically attack you and once the verdict is given, he'll have no cause to trouble you any further. But there are one or two things we can do. Do you have a telephone with caller identification?'

'No.'

'We'll have a word with the telephone people and ask them to install one and to put a trace on your line so that the number of any caller can be identified even if he rings on a phone that has been instructed not to disclose it. If you receive another threatening call, inform the exchange immediately, then us. Of course, a villain with the slightest intelligence will use a public call box, but we might be able to gain a definite lead. And as regards your safety, duty patrols will have orders to keep a priority watch on the house.'

'A moment ago, you said there was no chance of my being attacked.'

'Added pressure could be put on without that; chucking a brick through a window, that sort of thing. If any would-be chucker realises there's special police surveillance, he'll quickly forget the idea ... I think that's everything.' He stood.

Gregg accompanied them to the front door and said goodbye. He checked that all downstairs windows and doors were secure, went upstairs and set the alarms from the subsidiary controls, entered the bedroom.

Diana was in bed, reading a book. She did not look up.

'The police will arrange for any future calls to be traced and patrols will keep a special watch on us,' he said.

'Is that all?'

'What more can they do?'

'Post a permanent guard on the house.'

'As far as I know, that takes about eight men because of watches and reliefs and so ...'

'Didn't you demand someone here all the time?'

'I didn't, no.'

'Because you're too weak to demand anything.'

'Because they couldn't have agreed for the reason I've just given and because the value of the threat becomes nil if it's ever carried out.'

'Don't be so ridiculous.'

'I'm quoting the detective inspector.'

'He only said that to try to make you think the police were doing all that's necessary when they're really doing nothing.'

'It's logical.'

'Only if you're trying to cover up for yourself ... Why the hell didn't you keep quiet as you were told to; then we wouldn't have had all this terrible trouble?'

'You can't see that if Lipman did rape the woman, he must be found guilty and punished?'

'She probably asked for it.'

*   *   *

'What did you make of him?' Noyes asked as they left, driving northwards.

'Hard to say,' Duggan replied stolidly. 'Seemed straightforward enough.'

'In spite of introducing a German for extra colour? You don't think he might have added that what the man actually said was: "You vill suffer most 'orribly"?'

'How's that, sir?'

Noyes didn't bother to explain. He braked to a halt at lights and waited impatiently for them to change.

CHAPTER SIX

As he waited for the court to settle, the judge's lean, lined face expressed nothing of his thoughts, least of all when he glanced briefly at Lipman in the dock. 'Members of the jury,' he said, once there was quiet, 'I have been informed that one of you has received a second threatening telephone call, again demanding a certain verdict. Let me repeat that it is the duty of each and every one of you to reach a verdict solely on the evidence presented in this court; you must allow no other factor to weigh in your minds. In order that you can carry out this duty unhindered, the police have been instructed to maintain a careful watch and to prevent any further attempt to suborn your judgments.

'Very well, Mr Musgrove.'

Mrs Benson was called. She testified that when her daughter had arrived home on the night of the fourth of March, both she and her husband had been asleep, but her daughter's distress had awoken her.

'Please describe in your own words what happened when you went into her bedroom.'

Mrs Benson was nervous and embarrassed,

yet determined to give her evidence with all the force she could. 'I found Joyce lying on the bed . . .'

'Was she dressed?'

'Yes.'

'In the clothes she had been wearing when she left the house the previous evening?'

'Yes.'

'What did you do?'

'I asked her why she was crying and what was the matter. She couldn't speak, so I sat and cuddled her and tried to persuade her to tell me what was wrong.'

'Did you eventually succeed?'

'She told me . . .'

'I'm sorry, Mrs Benson, but your daughter will have to tell us that. As a result of what she said, did you make any suggestion as to what she should do?'

'I said the police must be told.'

'Did she agree to this?'

'Not then, no. She became hysterical, so I didn't say anything more about it.'

'What happened next?'

'I persuaded her to undress and get into bed whilst I made her a hot drink. She had a couple of aspirins with that—I hadn't anything else to give her. I stayed with her and eventually she fell asleep. In the morning, she was calmer and I was able to get her to agree to me phoning the police and telling them what had happened.'

'And you did so?'

'Yes.'

'As a result of what the police said to you, did you collect together the clothing your daughter had been wearing the previous night?'

'Yes.'

'And you handed this to a detective?'

'Yes.'

Musgrove turned and spoke to his junior, who spoke to their instructing solicitor behind him; the solicitor, thanks to being long and lean, was able to bend across the intervening row of benches and speak directly to Musgrove.

Musgrove turned back to face the witness box. 'Mrs Benson, do you welcome your daughter's bringing home her male friends?'

'Yes, of course.'

'Then you must have met a number of them?'

'Joyce has always been popular and . . .' She stopped suddenly and swallowed repeatedly; her expression portrayed the inner struggle to control her emotions.

Musgrove waited until she was once more relatively calm, then said: 'We have heard evidence that the first meeting between your daughter and the accused was last year. Did she mention this meeting at that time?'

'No.'

'Since then, has she introduced him to you?'

54

'No.'

'Has she ever mentioned him to you?'

'No.'

'Then you had no reason to know she had ever met him?'

'None.'

'Thank you, Mrs Benson.'

Yates rose as Musgrove sat. He was at his most urbane when he said: 'Would you imagine that you can be certain you have met every one of the male friends your daughter has known in the past five years?'

'Well, not certain, but . . .'

'You would agree, then, that she might have had male friends who, for one reason or another, she has not introduced to you?'

'If she really likes someone . . .'

'Please answer my question.'

She said firmly: 'If she really likes someone, she brings him home because she wants him to meet us and us to meet him.'

The reply displeased Yates. His tone sharpened. 'Does your daughter normally return home after she has finished work?'

'If she's not doing anything special.'

'And she has supper with you?'

'Of course.'

'Did she have supper with you on the evening of the fourth of March?'

'No.'

'But you were expecting her to do so?'

'Not after she phoned to say she wouldn't be

back until later.'

'Thank you.'

Musgrove, not bothering to stand, said: 'No further questions.'

* * *

Winifred Russell had used a great deal of make-up and dressed flamboyantly in order to try to bolster her self-confidence. After the preliminary questions had been put, Musgrove said: 'On the fourth of March, what did you do when you finished work?'

'We went to the Bull and Bear for a drink.'

'Perhaps you would clarify your answer. Who is "we"?'

'Me and Bert and Joyce.'

'And who is Bert?'

'Bert Fegan.'

'He is a friend of yours?'

She said hurriedly: 'My husband cleared off a year ago and I've not heard a word from him since, so . . . What I mean is. . .' She came to a stop.

'Mrs Russell, rest assured that your relationship with Mr Fegan does not concern the court. Does Mr Fegan also work at Dawkins Engineering?'

'Yes.'

'You have told us the three of you went to the Bull and Bear for a drink. Is the public house near your place of work?'

'It's in the same road.'

'Whose suggestion was it that you should go there after work?'

'I suppose it was Bert's; usually is.'

There was some laughter.

'And was it he who asked Miss Benson to join you?'

'I did. We met just outside the building and I said why didn't she come along as she was a bit down.'

'Meaning that she was not as cheerful as usual?'

'That's right.'

'Will you describe what took place in the public house?'

They'd found a table and she and Joyce had sat whilst Bert had gone to the bar for a half of bitter and two gins and tonic. They'd been chatting and drinking for a while when he'd walked in . . .

'Whom do you mean?'

'Him.' She looked briefly at the dock, her expression bitterly antagonistic.

'Mr Lipman?'

'Yes.'

'What did he do?'

'Went to the bar. Then he looked around, saw us, came over and said hullo to Joyce and she introduced him to Bert and me. He joined us.'

'At whose invitation?'

'No one's. He just sat down.'

'He invited himself?'

'That's right.'

'Were you expecting to meet him?'

'Course not. Like I said, me and Bert didn't know him.'

'Was it your impression that Miss Benson expected to meet him?'

'No way. She was surprised to see him.'

'What happened after he had joined you?'

'We talked, then Bert said we'd best be leaving because we was going to the flicks and so we left.'

'The three of you had only the one drink before you and Mr Fegan left?'

'That's right.'

Musgrove sat, Yates stood. 'Mrs Russell, did Miss Benson show any wish, either by word or action, to leave the public house at the same time as you did?'

'Not really.'

'She seemed perfectly content to remain there in the company of Mr Lipman?'

'I suppose so.'

'Thank you.'

*　　　*　　　*

They filed into the juryroom. The usher, with a sense of self-importance, said they must report on or before nine-fifteen the next morning and they were not to discuss the case with anyone.

'What do you think about things?' Sharman

asked in his reedy voice, as the usher left.

Was he asking in order to find out what he himself thought? Gregg wondered with amusement laced with scorn. 'It's surely a bit early days to judge?'

'I suppose it is.'

'Well, I don't suppose anything of the sort,' Hendry said, as he came up to where they stood. 'He filled her up with booze until she didn't know whether her legs were crossed or wide open and jumped aboard.' He put his mackintosh on after a slight struggle with the right arm.

Gregg said drily: 'The evidence so far is she drank one gin and tonic.'

Hendry tapped the side of his nose with his right forefinger. 'But we all know what happened after the other two left the pub.'

'There are those of us who lack sufficient imagination to visualise the evidence to come,' said the woman nearest to them before she turned away.

Hendry watched her leave the room. 'You know her problem? There's never been anyone wanting to buy her even one drink . . . Here, have you heard the latest one about the Prime Minister?'

'Probably,' Gregg replied.

Sharman found that amusing.

*   *   *

The evening was unexpectedly proving to be a success, Gregg thought, largely thanks to Carol who, from her arrival, had been generous with her compliments. Diana had a childlike appetite for praise.

Diana looked down the dining-room table. 'No more cheese for anyone? Shall we move, then?'

As they stood, Gregg asked what liqueurs each would like. Carol chose a green Chartreuse, her husband preferred another malt, if that was OK; Diana said the usual.

On the way out of the dining room, Diana said: 'Joe hasn't been out for a long time, so put her in the garden.'

'Will do,' Gregg answered.

Joe, remembering that chocolates were offered to guests, started to waddle after the other three. Gregg called and she stopped, turned her head and looked at him, then continued on her way. He picked her up and carried her through to the kitchen, put her down and opened the outside door; since she showed no desire to go out, he gently eased her with the side of his shoe.

He poured out the drinks, put the glasses on a silver salver, carried them through to the drawing room.

'You've heard we've been beaten hollow again?' Barnard said as Gregg handed him the whisky. 'Overwhelmed and humiliated.'

'The story of all our colonial wars of the last

century, even when we've won.'

'How's that?'

'It's only John trying to be funny,' Diana said, annoyed. 'He's got a ridiculous sense of humour.'

'Oh! Rather good, really.' He chuckled. 'I wonder what the Australian team would have to say at being called colonials?'

'Something very pithy and even more impolite.' Gregg sat.

'You know the trouble? The selectors are pig-headed ignoramuses. I could have told 'em that new fellow might be able to bat a little at county level, but put him up against test bowling and he wouldn't know his arse from his elbow. I saw him at the Oval when . . .'

Gregg warmed the glass of Armagnac in the palm of his hand and thought that listening about cricket was almost as boring as watching it. Carol said her husband had been captain of the first eleven at school and never got over the fact. School remained a poor preparation for the real world—it preached the virtues of honesty, humility, and acceptance of authority . . .

'John, are you going deaf?' Diana asked sharply.

'Probably.'

'Where's Joe?'

'You asked me to let her out.'

'And have you let her back in?'

He put his glass down and stood.

'I have a husband with a memory like a sieve,' Diana announced.

'His can't be worse than Henry's,' Carol said. 'Yesterday I asked him to be sure to post an important letter and he came back with it still in his pocket.'

'A dead letter,' Gregg said, as he left.

He opened the outside kitchen door, expecting to find Joe waiting, resentful at having been forgotten but willing to forgive at the price of a piece of chocolate biscuit. She was not there. He switched on the lights which illuminated half the lawn. Still no Joe. He whistled and called, but there was no response.

He returned into the kitchen to pick up a torch, went back and across to the far half of the lawn where he switched on the torch. He swung the beam round. 'Where the hell are you? Hurry up and appear or my Armagnac will have evaporated.'

A dog yapped, but even as he turned to his right he identified it as the miniature pinscher in the next garden. Joe and it were forever barking defiance at each other, their bravery bolstered by the fact that they never met. It was odd that Joe hadn't yapped back . . .

He began to worry; perhaps her collar had been caught on something or Althorpe had carelessly left a fork around with prongs pointing upwards . . . He hurried to the end of the lawn, crossed the gravel path and went round the hedge into the kitchen garden.

Because of the different heights of the growing plants, he had to search carefully, row by row. And it was not until he was past the runner beans that he saw a shadow against the rhubarb. As he approached, he willed it into dissolving, but the nearer he drew, the more definite form it gained; he had found Joe.

He hunkered down on his heels. The flesh was still warm, the mouth was open and her tongue, which hung out, had been bitten. A heart attack. Even though, four days before, Diana had so roughly rebuked him for giving Joe some chocolate biscuit, she'd fed her titbits throughout the day, every day. The vet had proved himself to be an accurate prognostician.

He stood, stared at Joe in the light of the torch. Diana had had her when they'd first met and even then had treated her with exaggerated affection. She'd demanded he propose to Joe as well as to herself. He had done so. Love was a form of insanity.

Diana was going to be so emotionally distressed that it must be better not to tell her about it until after Carol and Henry had left . . . Stupid thinking. If he returned to the house without Joe, Diana would immediately initiate a search. Her distress would surely be that much greater if she discovered the corpse. Better to move it and then, as far as was possible, prepare Diana for the news.

He went across to the shed, on the far side

of the kitchen garden, and found a sack. He returned, laid the torch on the ground, and went to pick up the body. Finding it seemingly more heavy in death than in life, he shifted his grip to gain a better balance and felt something prick his hand. He reached out and picked up the torch and directed the beam at where his hand had been. He saw a noose of wire which had been drawn tightly around the neck. She had not suffered a heart attack, she had been strangled.

CHAPTER SEVEN

Their doctor had a private practice, which explained why he'd been prepared to drive to their house late at night and examine, then treat, Diana. He spoke to Gregg in the hall. 'I've given her something to calm her down and put her to sleep and she should remain peaceful through the night. However, if she doesn't, give her two of these.' He passed across a small plastic pillbox. 'No more than two in six hours, whatever happens. I'll drop by in the morning to make certain everything's all right. There's no reason to suppose it won't be, even if she has reacted somewhat strongly to events.'

A tactful doctor's way of saying she'd reacted hysterically. Gregg opened the front door, shook hands, waited until the doctor had reached his car, parked in the road behind the CID Escort, then shut the door and crossed the hall to the green room.

Menzies was seated in one of the armchairs. 'How is Mrs Gregg?' he asked.

'The doctor's doped her and she's asleep,' he answered as he sat.

'Much the best.' Menzies looked down at his notebook. 'We'd covered almost everything before you had to have a word with the doc, so I won't keep you much longer . . . After finding the noose around the dog's neck, you undid it. Why?'

Gregg considered the question. 'I suppose it was instinctive. It just didn't seem right to leave Joe with it around the neck. Does that make sense?'

'Indeed, since I've a dog of my own. What did you do with the wire?'

'I stuffed it in the dustbin; I didn't want my wife to see it.'

'Before I leave, I'll retrieve it in case it can tell us something.'

'Killing Joe like that is meant to shock and frighten me, isn't it?'

'I don't think at this stage one can be certain it's connected with the telephone threats.'

'Who else could be so barbarous?'

'There are sad people who get their kicks out of doing that sort of thing.'

'It would be a hell of a coincidence if that's

why Joe was killed.'

'Contrary to what many people think, coincidences happen all the time.'

'As far-fetched as this?'

'Well . . . Perhaps not that often.'

'They really mean to break me.'

'I hope they won't succeed.'

'Hoping comes easily when it's someone else's neck at stake.' Gregg spoke angrily. 'The police were supposed to be guarding us. Some guard when this happens!'

'Mobile and foot patrols have been keeping a special watch on the house.'

'Except when needed.'

'I'm afraid it's a fact of life that limited resources mean a limited ability to guard any individual.'

'Unless he's a politician.'

'That breed's always known how to look after itself.'

'Do we now get a full-time guard?'

'That decision will be taken by someone much higher up the line than me.'

'What's the decision likely to be?'

'I just can't say.'

'In other words, it's unlikely.'

'Whatever happens about that, Mr Gregg, it's worth remembering something that's been said before. A threat is only valid all the time it's not carried out.'

'Murdering a dog isn't carrying it out?'

'However much that hurts emotionally, you

have not suffered physically.'

'The distinction seems over-fine.'

'I assure you it's very relevant.'

'I was assured that I'd no cause to worry because the police would be keeping a special watch.'

'We did our best.' Menzies stood. 'Someone will be along in daylight to look around the garden . . . One last thing, if you'll show me where the dustbin is?'

There were three sets of gates, the third still bearing a small metal plaque on which could just be read the words, 'Tradesmen's entrance No hawkers'. The dustbin was behind that and Menzies was able, in the light from the side of the house, to see the length of thin wire. He picked this out and dropped it into the sack, previously left by the middle gate, in which was the dead dog.

'What happens to the body?' Gregg asked.

'When Forensic have finished someone will be in touch with you to find out what you want done with it.'

'My wife will probably . . .' He didn't finish.

Menzies said: 'There's time to make up your minds. Good night, then.'

Gregg watched Menzies walk briskly on to the pavement and then along to the parked car, the sack swinging to his stride. As he drove off, Gregg heard the church clock strike midnight; he'd have judged it to be very much later. Emotion could prolong time almost to infinity.

He returned into the house, checked windows, doors, and the alarms, went upstairs to their bedroom. Diana was asleep, her bedside light still on. As he looked down at her, he wondered how long his coming day would prove to be.

*   *   *

'It's all your fault,' Diana said, lacing her words with venom.

'Can't you understand . . .' Gregg began.

'I understand that if you'd kept your mouth shut as you were told to, this wouldn't have happened?'

He sat on the edge of the bed, just outside the shaft of morning sunshine, and reached across to take hold of her hand; she snatched it away. 'I had to tell them about the threats.'

'You didn't.'

'It was my duty . . .'

'How can you be so cruel as to say it was your duty to see Joe murdered?'

'I didn't know that was going to happen.'

'They told you.'

'They threatened me, not Joe. I know it's terrible for you . . .'

'You don't know anything because you don't care. You always hated her and you're glad she's dead.'

'I did not hate her, I am not glad she's dead,

68

I'm as upset as you.'

'You're a poor liar.' She turned over so that her back faced him.

He stood. 'What can I get you for breakfast?'

'My God! It means so little to you that all you can think of is food!'

'It would do you good to eat something.'

'I'd choke. But you go away and have a wonderful meal. Why not? As far as you're concerned, nothing's happened.'

Downstairs, he put an egg on to boil, the coffee machine on another ring, and two slices of bread in the toaster. He looked up at the electric clock. He must leave the house in just under an hour, but Mrs Mabey—the daily—would arrive before then. She'd be in the house until one. Since he wouldn't be back until late afternoon, he must ask one of their friends to be with Diana during the afternoon. Judy was probably the best bet. Good-hearted, she was always willing to give a hand if she could.

* * *

'I would remind all present that nothing may be said or written beyond this courtroom which identifies, or reasonably might identify, the next witness. Any breach of this prohibition will be viewed with the greatest severity,' said the judge. He looked at prosecuting counsel

69

and nodded.

Musgrove stood. 'Miss Benson.'

Joyce Benson visibly flinched as she entered the courtroom, shocked by the intensity with which she was regarded, and as she stepped into the witness box, her lips were quivering. Had she not been suffering such mental distress, she would have been an attractive woman with light brown wavy hair, blue eyes, a shapely nose, a generous mouth, a long, graceful neck, and a compact figure. She stood, fidgeting with a button on her dress, her gaze fixed on the floor of the courtroom. Only the insensitive could miss the fear and humiliation she was suffering. She was handed the New Testament and she took the oath in a voice that was hardly audible.

'Miss Benson, you will have to speak up so that the court can hear you,' the judge said sympathetically, yet authoritatively.

Musgrove began the examination-in-chief. As was customary, the preliminary questions were put as leading questions to which there would be no objection.

'Is your name Joyce Muriel Benson?'

'Yes.'

'Are you twenty-four years of age and are you unmarried?'

'Yes.'

'Do you live at number twenty-three, Arlington Crescent, Candisford?'

'Yes.'

'Are you employed by Dawkins Engineering and do you work in their accounts office in East Shinstone?'

'Yes.'

'Will you tell the court when you first met the accused, Mr Lipman?'

Slowly, so that it seemed as if a force greater than her will was manipulating her, she turned her head to look for the first time at Lipman in the dock. Then, very hurriedly, she looked away and once more down at the floor of the courtroom.

'Was it before the night of the fourth of March?'

'Yes.'

'You really must speak up. Can you say how long before?'

She shook her head.

'Will you give your best estimate?' Musgrove said coaxingly. He was adept at persuading a frightened witness to give her evidence.

*   *   *

Detective Constable Anderson was not as miserably discontented as his appearance usually suggested, but that still left room for much sour envy. He stepped out of the car onto the pavement and stared at Ankover Lodge and thought that come the kingdom of the ordinary man, perhaps it would be he who lived in such luxury. He crossed the pavement, opened the middle gate, stepped onto the stone path. The front door was opened by a woman whose looks were unfortunate. 'Detective Constable Anderson, local CID.'

'What about it?'

Those who worked for the rich so often assumed the supercilious manners of the rich. 'I've come to have a look round the garden.'

'Who said you can?'

'Mr Gregg knows all about it.'

She shrugged her shoulders. 'If it's all right by him.'

She led the way through the hall and the kitchen—more equipment than in the local Dixons—to the back garden which was many times the size of his. It was surrounded by a high brick wall, but this could offer little hindrance to an agile person because it was not topped with broken glass or barbed wire. He walked down the right-hand gravel path, visually examining it for marks as he did so, past the cross-hedge to the kitchen garden. Here, he found further cause for resentment. He was justly proud of the vegetables he grew on his allotment, but compared to those growing here his were mere barrow produce. The likes of the Greggs would never dirty their hands, so they must employ a gardener and thus enjoy the fruits—vegetables—of another's hard labour. Money divided the world into them and us; them had all the fun, us had all

72

the pain.

His views on life might be ridiculously prejudiced, but he did not allow them to influence his work. He searched both kitchen garden and garden as thoroughly as if the property had belonged to someone who bought a pint down at the local. He found nothing; not a single footprint or other trace in the well-cultivated moist soil that either as a flower or vegetable bed bordered the brick walling.

He stood in the centre of the lawn. The intruder was on top of the wall. Would he risk jumping down in the dark? The flower beds between the walls and the gravel paths were too wide for him to be able to step over them—and how could he do that as he lowered himself?—so no matter whereabouts he had entered, he must have stepped on soil. So why weren't there any impressions? It was easy enough to erase those he'd made on entry, but how could he do that on leaving, when he'd have to lift his feet off the soil first . . .?

He checked the garden shed. It was unlocked. He wasn't surprised—the rich could afford to be careless about their possessions. Inside, there was a considerable amount of equipment and he examined a small rotavator that would have done wonders for his allotment. At the far end, hanging on a nail, was a coil of thin wire and visual judgment said it was the same size as that used to strangle the dog. One end was bright and in contrast to the rest of the wire which had been dulled by age, suggesting it had recently been cut. Above the work bench was a rack of tools and in this was a wire cutter with plastic-covered handles. He carefully lifted this out by the tips and wrapped it in one sheet of a coloured supplement that was lying on the floor.

Twenty-five minutes later, he reported to the detective inspector. 'I reckon he must have gone in from the back, sir, not just because the dog would be there, but also because the front is so open to the road. Chummy would have wanted as much cover as he could find, wouldn't he, sir?' An egalitarian, resentful of privilege, yet he acknowledged rank more openly and often than other members of the CID.

'Probably. So you say he climbed over the wall and waited for the dog to be let out, as it had to be sooner or later, grabbed hold of it or more likely enticed it with food, and strangled it. Then he left, climbing back over the wall. But how the hell did he avoid leaving any impressions?'

'I've been thinking about that, sir. I reckon it's just possible, despite the width of the soil, to run along the path to get sufficient momentum, turn and jump, and grab hold of the top of the wall; then it's just a case of pulling up.'

'You're talking about an Olympic gymnast.'

'The only alternative I can see is he took along gear which fixed to the top of the wall that enabled him to lean out with a rake, or something similar, and scratch the soil. In one place, the surface has been recently disturbed. Just looks like a bit of weeding had been done, of course.'

'You're saying now that however he worked it, he must have known exactly what the job was going to entail?'

'It certainly looks that way, sir.'

'Then he'd have had to case the area . . . All right.'

Anderson walked to the door, opened it, then stopped and turned. 'Nearly forgot. There was a pair of wire cutters in the garden shed and I brought them back. There's the chance they'll have dabs on 'em which could become useful when we have a suspect.' He left.

Unless there was a suspect, Noyes thought with sharp annoyance, the fingerprint department was very unlikely to agree to try to identify any print—the task was too laborious. For years, the police had been promised a computer system that would flip through thousands—or was it millions?—of prints in no time flat and pick out probable matches, but no system so far produced had been able to meet its claims . . .

It seemed more and more likely that the killing of the dog had been a carefully planned job, executed by an expert, aimed at callously increasing pressure on Gregg. Yet where was the motive for going to all this trouble and risk? He swore. He was missing something and still had not the slightest idea what that could be.

CHAPTER EIGHT

Yates faced the witness box. 'You have told us your first meeting with Mr Lipman in February was when he and another member of the security firm brought the wages to Dawkins Engineering. What were the circumstances of that meeting?'

'He was in Mr Better's office and when I went in . . .' Joyce began.

'Just one moment. Who is Mr Better?'

'He's the accountant and when the wages are brought in, he has to sign for them.' She had gained a measure of confidence and only occasionally now showed signs of the acute nervousness and sense of humiliation which she had suffered in her examination-in-chief. Those who could appreciate that her ordeal was really only just beginning felt further sympathy for her.

'Thank you.' As always, Yates made a point of initially being polite, even friendly. 'Did you have a specific reason for going into Mr Better's office?'

'When the money arrives, I always check it with him before he signs.'

'You both count it to make certain the right amount is there?'

'Well, not every note. We check the bundles against the requisition.'

'You have told us that Mr Lipman was in the office when you entered. Did you have a conversation with him?'

'We had a bit of a talk because there was a wait while Mr Better had a telephone call.'

'Who initiated the conversation?'

The question perplexed her.

'Did you speak to Mr Lipman first, or did he address you?'

She sensed, rather than appreciated, that her answer could have damaging implications. She said hastily: 'He spoke to me.'

'You are quite certain of theat?'

'Yes.'

'Do you usually wait for the other person to speak first?'

'If he's a man.'

'If I may say so, a refreshingly old-fashioned sense of social decorum.' Yates's words suggested approval, his tone, scepticism. 'What happened after the phone call was over?'

'He signed the acceptance and I left and went back to my desk.'

'We know the office in which you work is designed on the open plan and that to reach the outside door Mr Lipman and his companion had to walk through the area in which you worked. When he left, did he walk straight across to the door and leave?'

'He came across to my desk.'

'For any particular reason?'

'He asked me . . . He asked me if I'd like to go out with him.'

'What was your answer?'

'I said I wouldn't.'

'Did you explain why?'

'No.'

'Can you tell the court now what was your reason?'

'I had a steady boyfriend.'

'You had a steady boyfriend.' Yates, not allowed explicitly to suggest that she had had sexual experience, placed sufficient emphasis on the last two words to strengthen the inference the modern age so often drew. 'When did you next meet Mr Lipman?'

'When he brought the wages again.'

'Do you remember when that was?'

'No.'

'I will tell you. It was on the twenty-fifth of February. Did you speak to Mr Lipman on this occasion?'

'Only to say hullo to him when he said hullo to me.'

'Did you then still have a steady boyfriend?'

'Yes.' There was a catch in her voice which alerted many to what was to come.

'Was your friendship with him then as strong

78

as it had been previously?'

'I . . .' She gripped the edge of the box with both hands.

'It is a fact, is it not, that by the end of the month you were no longer seeing him?'

She was silent.

'You must answer the question,' the judge said.

'We . . . I . . . He was seeing someone else.'

'Then when on the fourth of March Mr Lipman again brought the wages to the office, you no longer had a steady boyfriend?'

'No,' she murmured.

'Did you talk to Mr Lipman on this occasion?'

'A little.'

'Who initiated the conversation?'

'He did.'

'Mr Lipman will say that after your first meeting he accepted that you didn't wish to be friendly, but that on this third occasion it was you who spoke first.'

'It wasn't like that.'

'After you left Mr Better's office, you returned to your desk. When Mr Lipman was on his way out, did he cross to speak to you?'

'Yes.'

'Because you had smiled at him?'

'I didn't.'

'He will say that you and he had a friendly conversation; so friendly that he repeated his previous invitation and although you again

79

refused it, your attitude suggested that the next time you met, you would probably accept.'

'I didn't suggest anything.'

'Mr Lipman is a very personable man, is he not, and many young ladies would be happy to accept an invitation of his?'

She shook her head.

'I put it to you that on this third visit, you encouraged Mr Lipman's interest because your friendship with your steady boyfriend had recently come to an end and you had decided that Mr Lipman would be a very acceptable replacement?'

'It wasn't like that at all.' She began to cry.

*   *   *

With that strange desire to maintain an established routine which gripped most people, each member of the jury sat in the same position at the table as on previous occasions, even when relations with a neighbour were far from cordial. The meal was no better, but no worse, than the last one.

Sharman, on Gregg's right, said little, nervously unwilling to enter into any conversation which might become contentious. Mrs Ingham, on Gregg's left, expressed her opinions on any and every subject loudly and forcefully.

Hendry, halfway down the oblong table, said: 'It's beginning to sound like she gave him the old come-on.'

'Rubbish!' snapped Mrs Ingham. 'He was being a typical pest and she wasn't strong enough to tell him so.'

'She's telling the truth,' said the youngest woman present, who used make-up to the point where it was difficult to decide where reality began.

'How d'you know?' Hendry demanded.

'You've only got to look at her to see she's not lying.'

'You know the definition of the perfect liar? A woman on her wedding night.'

'Why don't you keep your smutty mind to yourself?' demanded Mrs Ingham.

Gregg wondered if the evidence would ever play a part in the verdict they reached.

*   *   *

Yates seldom looked at his brief and when he did so it was often for effect; he had a mind which could store an immense amount of detail and recall it virtually word perfect. 'In your examination-in-chief, you said you were surprised to see Mr Lipman enter the public house on the evening of the fourth of March; that when he saw you, he came across; that he wasn't invited to join you at the table, but just did so. That's not an accurate account of the meeting, is it?'

'Yes.'

81

'Was your surprise genuine?'

'Of course it was.'

'It hadn't occurred to you that he might well be waiting outside your place of work since you'd shown your interest only that morning ...'

'I didn't show any interest.'

'And that when he saw you were with friends, he might have held back until the three of you entered the Bull and Bear, whereupon he followed you?'

'I don't know why he was there.'

'When he stood at the bar and ordered a drink, you smiled at him to indicate he was to join you.'

'He just came across.'

'Whereupon you introduced him to your friends.'

'I had to.'

'You don't think that had you not welcomed his company, you could easily have avoided the introduction?'

'I ... I'm not very good at that sort of thing.'

'After a while, your friends left. You did not go with them which you surely would have done had Mr Lipman's presence irked you. The truth is, isn't it, that you chose to remain in his company?'

'I ... I was feeling miserable. He made me laugh.'

'And what better recipe for a relationship? Did you have any more to drink after your friends had left?'

'I had another gin and tonic.'

'And then?'

'He said, "Let's eat somewhere," and I said yes because . . .' She stopped.

'Because you were enjoying his company. Did you leave the public house as soon as you'd agreed to have a meal together?'

'I rang home first to say I'd be late back.'

'You did not expect to return home very shortly after your meal was finished?'

'I meant, too late for supper.' Her voice rose. 'You're twisting the meaning.'

'Miss Benson, I, and the jury, can only judge the meaning from your words. Where did you go for a meal?'

'He suggested McDonald's in Frencham.'

'That is several miles from Candisford where you live, is it not?'

'He said everything they served there was better than anywhere else.'

'You knew he lived in Frencham?'

'He . . . he mentioned it.'

'On arriving at Frencham, did you go straight to McDonald's?'

'He said he had to go into his flat to check his answerphone to see if a friend had called.'

'Was it at Mr Lipman's suggestion that you stayed in his car while he entered the flat?'

'Yes.'

'What happened when he returned?'

'He said his friend had left a message that

83

he'd be phoning again and the call was so important he'd have to wait for it. He suggested I went into the flat.'

'He suggested. He left you to decide. And your decision was to go into the flat, was it not?'

Very conscious of the inference that would be drawn unless she could prevent this, she said urgently: 'It was getting cold in the car.'

'You were not wearing winter clothing?'

'Yes, but . . . I was just sitting.'

'You didn't ask Mr Lipman to start the engine so that the car's heater could warm the interior?'

'I . . . I didn't think to do that.'

'Perhaps because you welcomed the chance to go into the flat?'

'All I wanted was to be warm.'

'It did not occur to you that by choosing to go into the flat, you would in all probability send a message to Mr Lipman?'

'No,' she said violently. 'Why should it?'

'It is a little difficult in this day and age to credit any attractive young lady with such a degree of naivety as to need an answer to that . . . Will you describe what happened after you entered the flat?'

'We sat in the sitting room and he offered me a drink. I told him, I didn't want one.'

'Mr Lipman will say that, on the contrary, you asked for a gin and tonic, which he gave you.'

'That's not true.'

'Did Mr Lipman's friend phone?'

'No.'

'And as time was passing, Mr Lipman suggested eating in the flat. Did you agree to this?'

'I was very hungry.'

'Did you have wine with the meal?'

'Only a little.'

'Mr Lipman will say that you and he shared a bottle of red wine, drinking glass for glass.'

'It's another beastly lie.'

'After the meal was finished, did you ask to be driven home?'

'He said he'd make coffee. Only . . .'

'Yes?'

'He came and sat on the settee and kissed me . . .'

'Did you object?'

She did not answer.

'Did you object to his kissing you?'

'Not . . . not immediately,' she said, her voice trembling. She looked beseechingly at the judge, seeking the help she had always believed the law offered the innocent, met only impassive neutrality. She briefly shut her eyes.

'After a good meal, several drinks, and pleasant conversation, you considered his action to be quite normal?'

'I . . .'

Yates waited. After a while, he said: 'What happened next?'

'He . . . he tried to become familiar.'

'In what way?'

She shook her head.

The judge spoke. 'Miss Benson, you must tell the court what you mean by "become familiar".' It was impossible to realise from his manner that it was only with deep regret that he accepted witnesses sometimes had to be put on the legal rack in order to determine guilt or innocence.

Proving there was courage beneath the outward timidity, she said: 'He tried to feel my breast and when I managed to drag his hand away, he pushed it under my skirt. I asked him to stop, but he seemed to become crazy and he kept pulling at my pants until they tore. I struggled and managed to get free and run to the front door, but as I was opening it, he held a knife near my throat and said he'd kill me if I didn't let him do what he wanted. I was so terrified that . . . He forced me to go through to the bedroom; he made me take off all my clothes and said he knew I really wanted him to make love to me and I had to tell him I did.

'I again begged him to stop and he called me a . . . a cockteaser because I'd just said I wanted him and now I didn't. He told me he'd show me what happened to cockteasers. He hurt me and when I said so, he just laughed. As soon as it was over, he demanded I tell him how much I'd enjoyed it. I didn't until he picked up the knife . . . He said that if I'd enjoyed it so much, we'd do it again. When he fell asleep, I escaped from the flat.'

'Where did you go?'

'Home.'

'If you had been raped, as you claim, why didn't you go to the police?'

She lowered her gaze and stared straight at him and spoke with sudden, bitter scorn. 'You can't begin to understand. You don't care how a woman feels; how dirty, how hopeless. All I wanted was my mother. I couldn't talk to men who wouldn't understand.'

'That's right,' shouted a woman in the public gallery and glared at the usher who rebuked her.

Yates was annoyed that he had underestimated her resolve and had therefore not been prepared for so strong a defence of her own actions. 'Mr Lipman will say that when the meal was finished and you refused coffee, you made it obvious you would welcome his advances; that you returned his kisses with considerable passion; that when he felt your breast, far from trying to remove his hand, you held it more tightly against your body; that when he slide his hand under your skirt, you parted your legs; that you suggested going into the bedroom for sex; that afterwards, you told him how very much you'd enjoyed what had taken place . . .'

'He made me say that,' she shouted wildly. She began to cry again.

87

CHAPTER NINE

When Gregg returned home, Diana was in the kitchen, putting cut flowers into a vase. Knowing how proud of her arrangements she was, he said: 'They're attractive. Are they all home-grown?'

'Are you blind?'

'Presumably that means they aren't?'

'If you could be bothered to look, you'd know they're not. But you never bother about anything that doesn't directly concern you. You're not even in the least bit upset about Joe.'

'I'm as shocked as you.'

'You expect me to believe that when I know you never cared about her?'

'That's nonsense. I was fond of her.'

'Then why did you let it happen?'

'How could I prevent it when I didn't . . .'

She slammed the trimming scissors down on the kitchen table. 'You could have prevented it by not telling the police about the phone calls.'

'I had to.'

'Because it was your duty? You didn't stop to think, did you, that you owe me a duty, you owed Joe a duty? Of course not! We don't matter. Much more important for you to prove what a noble prig of a man you are.'

'If justice is to survive . . .'

'Don't give me any more crap about justice and civilisation. If there were any justice, Joe wouldn't be dead.'

'I know you're emotionally very upset . . .'

'You don't know anything about me because you don't care. All you worry about is your image. You must tell the police so that they think what a wonderful person you are.'

'If you'd been in court today, you wouldn't talk about justice like that.'

'Why not?'

'The woman who was raped was in the witness box, being cross-examined. The questioning must have been fair or the judge would have stopped it, but she was embarrassed and humiliated. If my telling the police about the phone calls helps her even just a little . . .'

'Are you, the great upholder of justice, saying she was raped before you've heard all the evidence?'

'No one could put such pain into words if she's lying.'

'How very emotional!'

'I've never before seen such mental suffering.'

'Obviously, her feelings are very much more important to you than mine are.'

'For God's sake . . .'

'You were warned, go to the police and we'd suffer.'

'That man said it would be I who suffered.'

'But it's not you who was strangled, it was Joe. Murdered because of you. Who's next— me? You don't know and you don't care. You're ready to sacrifice anyone in order to be seen to be noble.'

'I know you were unusually fond of Joe, but . . .'

'So you think it perverse to be fond of anyone but yourself?'

'All I'm saying is that you were so fond of her, her death has upset you more than you realise. How could I have had the slightest inkling that anything would happen to her?'

'By thinking of someone other than yourself for once.'

He argued no further. In her present mood, she was determined not to listen to common sense.

* * *

In Lipman's examination-in-chief, he agreed that he had been attracted to Joyce at their first meeting, but that she had rejected his attempt to initiate a friendship; however, on his third visit, when he'd not intended to make any advance, it had been she who had made the first move. She had then refused his invitation, but he'd accepted that there were still some women who did not wish to seem to be forward and used initial reluctance as a smokescreen. He had not been waiting outside

90

the offices of her firm on the fourth of March and followed her into the Bull and Bear, it had been pure chance which saw him enter the pub at the same time as she was there. Since she had been with friends, he would not have gone across to speak to her had she not smiled at him with an unmistakable invitation.

He had not invited her into his flat in case she got the wrong idea; however, when he'd returned to the car, she had said she wanted to go inside. They'd had drinks and a meal. He'd opened a bottle of Australian wine to go with the food and had been surprised that she'd drunk as much as he. Afterwards, he'd offered coffee, but she'd answered by patting the settee to suggest he join her there. He'd kissed her and she'd responded passionately. Yes, he had put a hand on her breast, but that was as far as he'd gone until she'd undone the buttons of her dress so that he could slide his hand inside. When he'd fondled her nipple, she'd kissed him even more passionately . . . she'd laughed when her pants tore . . .

She'd hugged him as they'd walked into the bedroom. He'd undressed her, she'd undressed him. They'd had sex. They'd had sex again. Her uninhibitedness had surprised him. Then, very regretfully, she'd said she must go because her parents were so stupidly old-fashioned they were always on at her not to stay out late in case that made the neighbours talk. He'd driven her back to Candisford, left her at the

91

top of Arlington Crescent so that her parents would think she'd returned by the last bus.

As God was his witness, he had never threatened her; most especially, not with a knife. Why should he have done so when she'd proved to be so eager; even the dominant partner? When he'd learned she was accusing him of having raped her, he'd been utterly gobsmacked. The only reason he could suggest for her incredible behaviour was that her parents had somehow learned she'd had sex that evening and because they had such ridiculous attitudes, she had told them that she had not done so willingly, whereupon, and much against her will, they'd insisted she told the police.

*   *   *

As a cross-examiner, Musgrove sometimes employed the gambit of suggesting the witness was proving to be a shade too clever for him. But such a course offered few benefits on this occasion due to the paucity of evidence other than that given by the two concerned—the police had searched the flat for the knife Joyce had described, but had failed to find it—and Lipman was unctuously ready to admit that he had been physically attracted to Joyce and he was smart enough to remain apparently respectful and even a little cowed.

Late Friday afternoon, the judge decided

closing speeches should not be given until Monday morning and he adjourned the court until then.

*   *   *

Because he'd spent the week in court, Gregg had to work over the weekend correcting galley proofs so that they could be returned to the publisher by the middle of the week. When he finished late Sunday afternoon, he stared at the staple-bound pages. Was it a good book? How did one define 'good'? A couple of years ago, he'd attended a literary lunch at which the speaker had said that she always read a book in bed because it made her sleepy. Perhaps this one would make more people sleepier than his last one.

He stood, stretched, crossed to the window and looked out at the garden. Friends were always telling Diana how wonderful it looked and she invariably basked in their praise, even when there was reason to doubt its sincerity. If he hadn't known her as well as he did, he'd have thought she suffered a degree of inner insufficiency.

He left the library and, hearing her voice, went into the breakfast room. Startled, she swung round, cordless phone to her ear. She stared wide-eyed at him for a moment, then regained her poise. 'I'll be in touch,' she said into the phone before she lowered it and switched it off.

'Sorry if I startled you,' he said.

'What d'you expect when you creep around the place?'

'I must buy some hobnail boots . . . Was that your mother?'

'Do I have to report on the identity of every person I speak to?'

'It's just if it had been she, I was going to ask whether her sciatica is better?'

'Lumbago.'

'Oh! Well at least I didn't confuse it with an ingrowing toenail . . . I've finished and need some fresh air. How about coming for a walk?'

'No.'

He remained cheerful in the face of her hostile attitude. 'According to the latest medical advice, a good brisk walk is like a certain tinned dog meat.'

'What on earth are you talking about?'

'It prolongs active life.'

'Won't you ever learn not to try to be funny? And who wants to prolong life when that just means more misery?'

He decided to risk exacerbating her mood and said: 'I'm sure it would ease the hurt over losing Joe if you found another dog to take her place. I looked in the small ads in this week's *Shinstone Gazette* and there's a litter of four Pekes, three bitches and one dog, eight weeks old, for sale. The advertisement says there are show champions on both sides, but there's a chance they'll overcome that disability. How about ringing and suggesting we drive over and look at the pups?'

'You don't understand people, do you?'

'Certainly not as much as I'd like to.'

'You really can think that I'd get another dog and just throw away all memories of Joe; that I could bear seeing another dog feeding from Joe's bowl, sleeping in her basket, playing with her toys?'

'Buy new feed bowl, basket, and toys . . .'

'How can you be so stupid?'

He left the house and walked down the hill to the park.

CHAPTER TEN

'You are the sole judge of fact,' the judge said to the jury as he neared the conclusion of his summing-up. 'It is your duty, and yours alone, to decide what evidence you believe and what evidence you disbelieve.

'In reaching your decision, you will remember that in order to bring in a verdict of guilty, you must be satisfied beyond all reasonable doubt of the guilt of the accused; merely to believe it probable he is guilty is not enough. As has been said, in this case much depends on whom you believe—Miss Benson

95

or the accused—since there is little direct evidence and you may hold, as counsel for the defence has asked you to, that the circumstantial evidence is ambiguous. To bring in a verdict of guilty, you must be convinced that Miss Benson was telling the truth when she said a knife was held to her throat in order to force her to have sex; that the police failed to find in the flat a knife which resembled her description does not lessen her credibility; that the accused was lying when he said Miss Benson welcomed and encouraged his advances and at no time prior to the full act of sex did she demand he stop.'

Ten minutes later, he told the jury to retire and consider their verdict.

* * *

'I'm not all that certain how we go about things . . .' Gregg began.

'Tell the old boy guilty so we can clear off home,' Hendry said with typical stupidity.

Gregg ignored the intervention. 'However, perhaps the thing to do is have a general exchange of views and then a ballot.'

'That sounds reasonable,' said the nearest woman to him.

'Shall I start?'

No one objected.

'As the judge said, since the two versions of what happened in Lipman's flat are in total opposition, everything depends on which of the two we believe. To answer that, it may help to remember what each claims happened at their first meeting. She said he was in Better's office when she entered and she did not speak to him, it was he who spoke to her first . . .'

'Hardly a point of much substance.' Akers was a thin, balding, pedantic man who on previous occasions had said little or nothing. 'Even in these regrettably free and easy times, it is usually the man who makes the first approach.'

'The significance I see here is the way in which she told us he had initiated the conversation. I gained the immediate impression that she is a naturally modest, retiring kind of person.'

'Or adept at seeming to be so.'

'What makes you say that?' demanded Mrs Ingham, with her customary belligerence.

'Because we were specifically told by the judge to consider all possibilities before coming to a conclusion.'

'When Lipman left, he made a point of going over to her desk,' Gregg said, 'and he asked her to go out with him. She refused because she was friendly with a man. By refusing, she showed a sense of loyalty.'

'Or that she wasn't a smart enough fiddler to play two fiddles at the same time,' said Hendry.

'We'll get along much more quickly if you

stop saying things like that,' snapped Mrs Ingham.

'Yeah,' agreed Miss Cameron. 'And if you think you're funny being sexist, you couldn't be more wrong.'

Gregg spoke quickly to prevent any further ill-will. 'On the second visit, Lipman was again the first to make contact.'

'According to her, but not to him,' contradicted Akers. 'I thought we were trying to decide who is the liar? You are assuming from the start that he is.' He had a voice which coated every word with dust.

'I am accepting that being the kind of woman she is, she would not have made the running.'

'But isn't the question, what kind of a woman is she? If she's adept at lying, she is not the woman you are assuming her to be.'

'That has to be right,' agreed Sharman.

Gregg was surprised that Sharman should not only offer an opinion, but one that was clearly against the general opinion.

*   *   *

'I think it's time to have a ballot,' Gregg said.

One or two nodded their agreement, the rest waited.

'How many vote guilty?'

Ten hands were raised.

'Not guilty?'

Akers raised his hand; after a pause, Sharman nervously raised his.

'A majority of ten to two is good enough,' Hendry said, 'so let's go back in and tell 'em and get it over and done with.'

'I think we should go over all the important points once again, to make certain,' Gregg said.

* * *

'It was all lies,' Mrs Ingham said. 'He had no intention of having a meal at the local McDonald's and there wasn't any expected phone call. All that was to get her into his flat.'

'Where is the proof of such assertions?' Akers asked.

'You need proof?' Miss Cameron spoke scornfully. 'You ain't seen much of the world, that's for sure!'

There were murmurs of agreement.

Akers seemed unperturbed. 'We really must not prefer imagination to fact. The fact is that on her own admission Miss Benson willingly entered the flat.'

'Because she was cold. And he made sure she was cold by telling her the car heater didn't work.'

'You have just proved my contention.'

'What's that supposed to mean?'

'That all too little regard is being given to the facts. There was no mention by her of a

99

broken heater.'

'Then why was she so cold?'

'She said, because the engine was not running to power the heater.'

'Where's the difference?' she asked with added belligerence.

'My dear young lady, if you can't—'

'I am not your dear young lady,' she said furiously.

* * *

'I suggest we have another ballot,' Gregg said wearily.

Several nodded; Mrs Ingham said it would be the last if only certain people could see sense.

Again, ten voted guilty, Akers and Sharman voted not guilty.

Gregg was not surprised that Akers should continue to vote as he did—having reached a decision, he'd refuse to change it, come hell, high water, or common sense; he was surprised that Sharman should do so—he appeared to be someone who would always strive to be with the majority. He turned to Akers. 'Is there any particular part of the evidence you'd like to discuss again?'

'I'd like to ask why so many of you are ignoring what the judge said?'

'In what context?'

'That we must reach a verdict on the facts

and only on the facts; that if there is the slightest doubt in our minds, we must bring in a verdict of not guilty.'

'I'm sure we're all remembering that.'

'Really? I'd have said that most of you are making two assumptions which are not supported by the facts.'

'And those are?'

'That she would never be the first to initiate a friendship; that she would never subtly make it clear she would welcome the friendship's becoming intimate.'

'The circumstantial evidence supports both contentions.'

'Circumstantial evidence demands that assumptions be drawn; assumptions are not evidence.'

'I have heard it said that circumstances cannot lie, persons can.'

'Like most popular sayings, close examination shows it to be fatuous.'

'If the circumstances all point to one conclusion, you would not accept that that conclusion is fact?'

'Assumptions can become facts only to a blinkered mind . . .'

'What is the use of going on like this?' demanded Mrs Ingham. She leaned forward as she glared at Akers. 'Are you too blind to see she was telling the truth?'

'Is there, then, some physical sign I don't know about which positively identifies a person as being invariably truthful?'

'You may talk clever,' said Miss Cameron, 'but you ain't no Einstein when it comes to people.'

'Shall we have the ballot?' said Gregg.

'Yeah.' Hendry's voice rose. 'And if there are still two who can't see their noses in front of their faces, I say we go back into court and tell 'em there's ten of us shouting guilty.'

Even Mrs Ingham nodded her agreement.

*   *   *

The judge said: 'Is it possible that if you return to the juryroom and consider the matter further, you may reach a unanimous verdict?'.

Gregg, standing, answered. 'I am afraid there is very little likelihood of that.'

'Very well. Since you tell me that ten of you are in agreement, the court is empowered to accept a majority verdict. What is your verdict?'

'Guilty, my lord.'

CHAPTER ELEVEN

Diana met Gregg in the hall. 'Well?'

'Guilty.' He shut the front door.

'Christ! What's going to happen to us now?'

'There's absolutely no need to worry.'

'What a bloody fool you can be! No need to worry when they murdered Joe?'

He moved forward to give her a reassuring hug, but she stepped back. 'Their threat was only valid all the time . . .'

'For God's sake, don't give me that again.'

'I know I keep saying it, but it is logical. Why should they do anything now when nothing can alter the verdict?'

'Why did you find him guilty?'

'In the witness box, she was obviously speaking the truth, he was lying to save his skin.'

'Then the verdict would have been the same if you'd never told the police about the threats?'

'I suppose that's one way of looking at things.'

'But you had to show what a good citizen you are.'

'I know it's been tough on you . . .'

'Why d'you keep telling me you know how things have been for me, when you don't bloody know? You had no idea how I suffered when Joe was murdered. You haven't given a damn what it's been like for me to sit here, dreading what's going to happen.'

'And nothing more will, so relax. I always try to take a break between books, so let's take off in a car for somewhere; it'll do you a power of good.'

'No.'

'A complete change of scene . . .'

'Mother rang earlier. She's not very well. I'm going now to see her. I don't know when I'll be back.'

'Would you like me to go with you in case it's very late before you can get away?'

'No.'

'Well, you do have the mobile in the car so in case of any trouble . . .'

'I'll try to find someone who can help, not drop me into something worse.' She crossed to the stairs and climbed them.

He sighed. There were none so blind as those who found pleasure in not seeing. He went through to the larder and poured himself a drink. He felt mentally exhausted. When, in court, he'd said 'Guilty' he'd clearly appreciated that he was destroying a man's existing way of life. It had been an exercise of power he hadn't sought and wished he had not had because it had been a bit too close to playing God, but which it had been his duty to carry out.

He finished the first drink, poured himself a second one, left. He reached the hall as she opened the front door. She looked back. 'Your car's in the way.'

'I'll move it.'

He put the glass down at the side of the telephone and went past her and out to the Ford. As was becoming the case, the engine was reluctant to fire, but eventually he got it going and backed out into the road. She drove off in the Mercedes without even a goodbye wave of the hand. Her moods were becoming ever blacker. A visit to her mother was not going to lighten them . . .

Back in the house, he collected up his drink and went through to the green room, sat, picked up one of the magazines on an occasional table. As he leafed through it, he read about an offer, sponsored by the magazine, for a mini-holiday in Cochem, with one day spent aboard a riverboat. Years ago, he'd briefly visited the town and loved it for its fairy castle, the river, and the draught Moselle. Five days there would surely ease away at least some of Diana's nervous fears and allow them to regain a reasonable relationship?

*   *   *

He had cooked himself supper in the microwave and was eating in the kitchen when the phone rang; he crossed to the wall on which an extension hung.

'Mother's bad,' Diana said, not bothering with any form of greeting.

'I'm very sorry to hear that. The sciatica's much worse, then?'

'Lumbago. I told you last time.'

'Yes, of course. After a certain age we start to lose our brain cells and mine are departing at twice the normal rate . . . Has her doctor been able to help?'

'The man she usually sees is in hospital and the bitch of a receptionist had the nerve to tell me that all the other partners were very busy because he was away and it might not be possible for anyone to call immediately. So with the state she's in, I can't leave her on her own and I'm staying the night.'

'Of course. Don't ring off yet.'

'What is it?'

'Remember I suggested that a break away from here would do us both a world of good? I was looking through a magazine and in it is an offer for five days in Cochem, one of which is spent on the river. It's an attractive part of the country. How about going there?'

'You think I can worry about holidays now?' She cut the connection.

He returned to the table and resumed eating. As was the way of life, now that they would not be spending five days in Cochem, the desire to do so became greater . . .

The phone rang again.

'How's my favourite married man?' Anne asked.

'Longing to see you again.' She was happily divorced, bubbly, vivacious, and they enjoyed a flirtatious friendship that never had, and never would, go any further than words.

'Then, lucky man, your longings are going to be fulfilled.'

'*All* of them?'

106

'Unless you're thinking of writing a postscript to the *Kama Sutra* ... I want you and Di to come to dinner on the twentieth. Some people have recently moved into the area and you'll enjoy meeting them. He's just like you.'

'Suave, handsome, and irresistible?'

'Stop being so hopelessly optimistic. So you'll come?'

'I'll have to check with Di.'

'Then do that while I hang on.'

'She's with her mother so I'll have to ring her there and get back on to you.'

'Can't you consult her social diary?'

'I only read the diaries of people who don't know me for fear of learning some home truths ... She does keep a note of invitations, but often forgets to put one down, so I'll have to check with her first if I'm not to end up in her black book.'

'You poor lamb.'

'Then remember the advice on how to enjoy a truly contented life.'

'I'll buy it.'

'Rise with the lark and bed with the lamb.'

She had a throaty laugh that suggested many things. 'Tell Di from me that if you have a previous engagement, you're to cancel it.'

A few minutes later they said goodbye and he replaced the receiver. He could never remember Susan Grantley's number—no doubt, deliberately—and had to look it up before he phoned. 'It's John.'

'John who?' she asked.

As if she didn't know! 'Son-in-law John. Has one of the doctors been to see you yet?'

'What are you talking about?'

'Your lumbago.'

'What about it?'

'Diana said it was so bad that she's staying with you and your usual doctor is ill in hospital and it's proving very difficult to get one of the other partners to visit you at home.' He waited, but she said nothing. She often complained to Diana that she couldn't understand half of what he said. 'Might I have a word with Di?'

'She's not here.'

'Not? Has she had to go out to get you something to try to ease the pain, then?'

After a while, she said: 'That's right.'

'Then will you ask her to ring me when she returns? ... Good night, Susan, I hope you'll soon be very much better,' he said, with a touch of malice, knowing that she disliked his calling her by her Christian name.

She did not bother to thank him for his good wishes.

He finished the meal, now barely warm, stacked the dirty things in the washing-up machine and left the kitchen to go through to the television room. He switched on the set. Coincidentally, the programme featured the Rhine and ended with a view of the Lorelei, to the accompaniment of Wagner. He decided that when Diana returned home, he'd again broach the possibility of a trip to Cochem.

The news began. It was mostly bad because the joys of life usually made weak television. It was followed by a documentary on society's problem of an ageing population that was increasing while the ability to meet its needs was declining. Since every passing second meant he was a second older, he turned the television off. He looked for the day's *Times*, but it was not in sight. Diana had a thirst for tidiness that was almost a mania, so he went through to the kitchen and in the scullery found the day's copy of *The Times* on top of a pile of newspapers that was ready to be taken to the council dump. He retrieved it and returned to the television room.

He read the three leaders, skimmed the letters, glanced at the obituaries. He checked the time. Almost eleven, which made it virtually certain Diana was not going to phone him that night. Because she'd been too occupied looking after her mother, or because her mother had not bothered to relay the message? Ten to one on the latter.

CHAPTER TWELVE

Because he was in the study, writing letters, the first he knew of Diana's return was when he heard her voice in the hall. He went through to there. She was talking to Mrs Mabey, who had reverted to a hairstyle that made it seem she had left her hairdresser halfway through the styling.

'Hullo, love,' he said.

'Must you?' Diana snapped.

He'd momentarily forgotten that the endearment 'Love' was one she abhorred; for her, it suggested north country grocers. 'How's your mother this morning?'

'All right.'

'What did the doctor say?'

'How would I know?'

'You sound as if you had a heavy night!'

'Why d'you say that?' She noticed that Mrs Mabey was regarding them with considerable interest and made for the breakfast room, indicating to him to follow. As he entered, she said: 'Shut the door.'

He did so.

'I suppose you've never heard of *pas devant les domestiques*?'

'There was hardly a day at home when it wasn't chanted over the cornflakes.'

'Your humour's fifth form.'

'At least I'm enjoying a slight promotion. The last time, it was fourth form.'

'You make me want to . . .' She stopped.

'Di,' he said quietly, 'if you're so terribly worried about your mother . . .'

'I'm worried that I come home and you

110

suggest I'm looking a mess in front of a servant.'

'Come off it. All I suggested was, you're obviously very tired. Having spent the night coping with your mother, that's hardly surprising.'

'Now you're going to rubbish her, I suppose?'

'I am not rubbishing anyone. If she's suffering hell from lumbago, you can't have had much sleep and you've every reason for being tired out.'

'Why did you phone me last night?'

'Then your mother did remember to tell you!'

'You were spying on me.'

'I was doing what? I'd say your sense of humour isn't sixth form either.'

'Were you trying to spy on me?'

'Why on earth should I do that?'

'That's no answer.'

'I phoned because I wanted to tell you that Anne's invited us to dinner on the twentieth to meet a couple who've moved near her. It was no good my saying yes without checking with you that you hadn't forgotten to write down some previous invite.'

She said nothing.

'Go on up to bed and have a sleep,' he said with quiet sympathy.

'I . . .' She stopped.

'Shall I be gallant and carry you at the risk

111

of a double hernia?'

'I'm sorry if I'm being a bitch. Forgive?'

'I would if, due to my excessive loss of brain cells, I could remember what it is I'm supposed to forgive.'

She came forward and kissed him lightly. 'Wake me up in time to get lunch.'

'Let's eat out? That way, you can sleep for longer.'

'You're so kind,' she murmured just before she left the room.

He put his hands in his trouser pockets and jingled some coins as he crossed to the window and stared at Althorpe, who appeared to have gone into a trance in front of a rose bush that was not blooming as well as in the past. It was strange that Diana should accuse him of trying to spy on her when she must be certain that his sense of loyalty was such that he could never believe the circumstances would ever arise when there could be cause for his spying. She must be even tireder than she looked.

*   *   *

On the morning of the nineteenth, they had just finished breakfast when Gregg said: 'There's something I need to check out and the reference books in the local library aren't sufficiently comprehensive, so I thought I'd drive into Shinstone and try the main library— they've a much better reference section. Is there anything you want while I'm there?'

'Barbara's asked me to coffee, but I forgot I'd arranged to have the car serviced. Will you drive it to the garage? They need it for the day, so I could use your car to go to her and then pick you up.'

'Fine. A couple of hours should be enough.'

'Then I'll leave her place at half-past eleven.'

'And you'll meet me at the library or will somewhere else be easier?'

'The library. There's usually parking space there.'

'By the way, the Ford's become reluctant to start. I've been meaning to get the local garage to sort things out, but haven't found the chance. Just keep churning the starter over and eventually it'll fire.' He collected up the plates, knives, cups and saucers, butter and jam dishes, sugar bowl, milk jug, and coffee pot, and put them on the tray.

Twenty minutes later, he drove off in the Mercedes. He enjoyed the fifteen miles to Shinstone, being a car enthusiast—his particular dream was an Aston Martin—and would have welcomed the chance to handle the Mercedes more often, but normally she took the wheel.

He left the car at the garage, walked to the main library. His research followed the not unusual course of false trails, dead ends, and contradictions, but eventually he uncovered

113

the information he wanted.

There was a café attached to, but independent of, the library and half a dozen tables, with chairs, had been set out in front of it; to add to the Continental image, there were sun umbrellas. He sat at one of the unoccupied tables and asked the young waitress for a coffee and a doughnut.

The doughnut was crisp and tasty, the coffee aromatic, the sun warm, and the passing women wore colourful summer dresses. His mind wandered back to the year of his money-strapped tour when he'd still been naive enough to believe that experience would enable him to write the great novel that every would-be author imagined was within himself. Towards the end of June, he'd arrived in Alassio and found a small hotel, at the back of town, which he could just afford. Birgitta had been a fellow guest who might well have launched two thousand ships in a different age. On the second night, she'd come into his room to ask him to go out for the evening. He'd been so astonished that she'd laughed, showing white even teeth—were all English boys so slow? For one week he'd enjoyed such passion that to remember was to doubt. Then she'd casually said she was leaving. His fervid pleas to her to stay because without her life would cease to have meaning had provoked brief, questioning pity. Didn't he yet realise that life only had meaning in change? His last sight of her had been of a smile of expectation. For many nights, he'd imagined her new partner and suffered jealous pain . . . It had been an experience that should have fuelled a novel, but ironically he'd never been able to bring himself to use it.

A blast from a car's horn jerked him back to the present and he looked at his watch. A quarter past twelve. Diana had obviously not left at half eleven, but that was hardly surprising; when she was with Barbara, they could talk the forelegs as well as the hindlegs off a donkey. He ordered another coffee; when the waitress asked him if he'd like another doughnut as well, he first said no, then changed his mind.

His face was now in full sunshine; Alassio had been filled with sunshine for a week. Gather ye rosebuds while ye may. He'd gathered a few, but it was only Birgitta who really fuelled his memories. Had she continued to live life at the limit until she'd exhausted it? Or had she returned to Sweden, married the boy next door, and settled down to humdrum stability?

A church clock struck once and he assumed that marked the half-hour, but his watch showed one o'clock. He began to worry. However interesting their gossip, Diana surely must have realised time was passing? Could she have forgotten she was picking him up in Shinstone? Hardly, since she was driving the

Ford. Perhaps the car had broken down? The mobile phone had not been in the Mercedes so she must have it with her and there'd be no difficulty in calling for help . . .

There was a public call box nearby and from it he would be able to watch the main entrance of the library. He paid the bill, crossed to the phone, inserted a card, dialled home. There was no answer. He dialled the mobile. No answer. He dialled Barbara.

'It's John. Is Di still with you?'

'She's not been here.'

'She said she was having coffee with you.'

'That's what we arranged. I suppose she's forgotten.'

'She can't have done. When I left home earlier, the agreement was that she'd have coffee with you before she drove here to pick me up.'

'I imagine you've rung home?'

'Yes. And tried the mobile.'

'Perhaps you managed to settle on different meeting places and she's stamping her feet somewhere else. Ben and I keep doing that. It's invariably his fault.'

'She knew I'd be at the library . . . Would you do something for me? Nip over to our place and see if you can learn anything?'

'Sure. The old man's not coming back to lunch today so I can put my grub on the back burner.'

'Couldn't be a worse time to ask. Sorry

116

about that.'

'No panic. Shall I phone you to tell you what the situation is?'

'I'm using a call box so it'll be best if I get back to you. In quarter of an hour?'

'Right.'

The fifteen minutes was spent in willing the battered red Escort to appear. He had to wait to use the phone. 'Any luck?' he asked as soon as the call was answered.

'John, you . . . Get back here right away.'

'What's happened?' he said hoarsely.

'You must hurry,' she said and cut the connection.

*   *   *

As the taxi started to climb Adeane Road, Gregg could see the police car, the recovery vehicle, and the knot of people, by the very sharp bend. Until now, he had been able to keep his worst fears at bay by assuring himself, even as he pictured ever more catastrophes, that his imagination was once again proving a traitor. But now all evasion became impossible.

'Stop here,' he said, his voice almost unrecognisable even to himself.

The taxi stopped. He opened the door and began to walk towards the section of Armco barrier that had become twisted.

'Hey, what about the fare?' shouted the taxi driver.

He continued, oblivious to everything but the horror that must surely lie ahead. Then his arm was gripped. 'Just stay back with the rest of 'em.' The police constable's tone was contemptuous.

'I've got to see what's happened.'

'There's nothing to see, not even for the likes of you.'

'Is it a red Ford?'

The PC's manner abruptly changed. 'What's your name, please?'

'For God's sake, let me through.'

'Your name, please, sir.' The PC was politely firm.

'Gregg.'

'Just wait a moment.'

He stood there, certain and yet, incredibly, still struggling to hope.

The taxi driver came up to where he stood, said belligerently: 'Suppose you give me the fare, mate?'

'What's that?'

'Eleven quid because you promised extra. Hurry it up.'

The PC returned and had a brief word with the driver, then said to Gregg: 'Would you pay the driver; he says you owe him eleven pounds?'

Gregg brought the wallet from his inside coat pocket and found it extraordinarily difficult to know what notes to choose. He handed over the fare.

'Thanks, guv,' said the taxi driver, trying to make up for his previous aggressiveness.

A second PC walked up to where they stood. 'Would you come this way, Mr Gregg.'

He followed the other past the recovery vehicle to the Armco barrier. Fifteen feet below, on a lawn, lay his crumpled Escort, surrounded by broken glass; one wheel had been wrenched free and was a dozen feet away. 'Where's my wife?'

'She's been taken to hospital. I'm afraid she was badly hurt.'

He could judge from the other's tone that she was dead.

CHAPTER THIRTEEN

Menzies entered Park's room. 'Sarge, the report's through from Vehicles on the Ford.'

Park's mind was a long way away—on the following Sunday, when he'd been given two tickets for the one-day county cricket match. 'What Ford?'

'The one in which Gregg's wife was killed.'

'Yeah. Of course. Poor sod.' He might have been commiserating with either the dead wife or the bereaved husband.

'Guess what?'

'If I want to play quiz games, I turn on the telly.'

'It wasn't an accident. The brake lines were tampered with to make 'em fail when the brakes were applied hard.'

Park considered the news for several seconds. 'How sure are they?'

'You know Vehicles.'

'But did you ask them if they're dead certain?'

'I did. And received an earful for impertinence.'

'What about a written report?'

'With us as soon as possible. Next year, maybe.'

Park watched Menzies leave. He tapped on the desk with his fingers. No matter what Vehicles' reaction might be to another request for confirmation, if he didn't make it, Noyes would have his nuts for marbles. He checked the number, dialled it. 'DS Park, C Division. Re the fatal red Ford Escort, how certain can you be that the brake lines were deliberately tampered with?'

'Goddamnit, it's not ten minutes since I was telling one of you blokes . . .'

'I know. But the DI ordered me to check.'

Rank had its usual effect. The speaker said there could be no doubt—not even in a DI's tiny mind. The lines had been deliberately weakened to the point that when the brakes were applied with considerable force, they must fail. Since the car had been driven down a steep road at speed and there had been a very sharp right-hand bend, the sequence of events could be plotted beyond any contradiction. The driver had gone down the slope faster than was advisable and had braked hard; the brakes had momentarily bitten, then they'd begun to go soft. In these conditions, an expert driver would realize what was happening, would react immediately, and with the skilful use of gears and handbrake might be able to avoid a crash. The average driver would put more pressure on the brake pedal and that would cause the brakes to fail completely. The car had hit the Armco barrier at considerable speed and at a sharp angle; momentum had somersaulted it over the barrier and down the hillside to land upside down in the garden below. Even if the driver had been wearing her seat belt, she would have suffered very severe, probably fatal, injuries . . .

Park wondered what the DI was going to say to the news.

*   *   *

'Shit!'

Park stood slackly in front of the desk.

'They're certain?' Noyes asked.

'According to them, it's more certain than yesterday's winner of the three o'clock.'

'A murder case is just what we didn't need.' Noyes rubbed the lobe of his right ear. 'Common sense says it's connected with the attempt to suborn Gregg when he was on jury duty. Experience says no villain is going to look for revenge when the risks involved are high and the job that's been missed could only have been small. Agreed?'

'All along the line, guv.'

'Why was she driving her husband's car and not her own?'

'She'd fixed for hers to be serviced at the main Mercedes agents, he was going to Shinstone in the morning to do some research at the library, so he took her car and left her his.'

'A switch that almost certainly couldn't have been expected, which seems to confirm he had to be the target . . . that house wouldn't leave much change from four hundred thousand to buy. They employ a daily and a gardener. His books must sell very well.'

'I wouldn't have thought so.'

'You've read 'em?'

'You know how it is when you meet someone who does something a bit unusual— you kind of get interested in what it is he does. I took a couple of his books out of the library and tried to read 'em. Trouble is, there's no real action and everyone seems to spend most of their time asking themselves why they're doing what they are and what it all means. The quotes on the jackets are good, but that sort of stuff definitely isn't my cup of tea.'

'Doesn't sound the kind of novel the

ordinary punter will go for.'

'I reckon it's more for the high foreheads.'

'Then the odds are it's not his books which provide the money. Either he's got loads of capital or she has. That the Merc is hers, while his car is an old banger, suggests the latter.'

There was a silence, during which Noyes stared out of the window. 'Tom,' he said slowly, 'does this crash ring any bells in your mind?'

'Can't say it does.'

'I'm sure that some time ago there was a report of a crash engineered by messing around with the brake lines. We've not had such a case and there's not been one listed on the monthly reports from county . . . See if any of the lads can put a finger on it.'

'Right, sir.'

Park left and went along to the CID general room. Duggan and Menzies were dealing with the paperwork that was always threatening to overwhelm everyone. 'Have either of you recently come across any reference to a case where a car's brakes were tampered with so it crashed?'

'I reckon so, Sarge,' Duggan said.

'When and where?'

'Couldn't say exactly. I just remember reading about an attempted murder in the paper and thinking how stupid it was to give all the details.'

'What d'you mean?'

'You know how papers sometimes print diagrams to show how things work? Yesterday it was the asteroid belt and how maybe one swung out and hit the Earth and killed off the dinosaurs . . .'

'D'you think we could stay with us humans? What about the brake job?'

'There was a diagram showing how the brakes had been sabotaged. Even to which part of the lines was most susceptible. As I said to Muriel, "This is going to give people ideas."'

'What paper was this in?'

'Can't rightly remember.'

Because the DI was in conference with the Superintendent, it was over half an hour later before Park was able to report to him.

'He can't name the paper?' Noyes asked.

'I've had him trying hard to place it, but no go.'

'Probably one of the tabloids.'

'I don't think you can be that certain, not with Mike. He's a great poetry lad.'

Noyes sat back in his chair. 'Reading about that could give a man ideas; especially a man with a wealthy wife . . . I'm wondering. I'm just wondering if maybe we're beginning to discover why nothing seemed to add up when Gregg reported he was being threatened to make him fix the jury verdict . . . We'd better start learning a lot more about him, only to start with it'll have to be done softly, softly.'

*   *   *

The phone rang; Gregg picked up the cordless receiver, switched it on.

'John, Eric and I want you to know how desperately sorry we feel for you. Di's always been so alive . . .'

He listened and wondered how Vera could believe that her words would comfort. As Diana's admirable qualities were listed and then extolled, he suffered an increasing guilt. If she really were so perfect, then every disagreement, every bitter argument, must have been his fault.

'You'll come and have a meal with us, won't you?'

'I'd like to a bit later on.'

'It'll just be the three of us because I'm sure that's how you'd prefer it.'

'Indeed.' We don't want our friends to be embarrassed by your grief . . .

'Are you sure you're all right?'

What would she say if he said no? 'Yes, thanks.'

'You will let us know if there's anything, anything at all, that we can do, won't you?'

'I will. You're very kind.'

'One must help when one can. Goodbye, dear John.'

There had been a catch in her voice as she spoke the last three words. She forever played to the audience; probably it was only lack of the slightest talent that kept her out of the Old Vic. He put the phone down after switching it off. He looked at his glass to find it was empty, picked it up, went through to the larder and poured himself the fourth gin and tonic of the evening. It was often said that a funeral was cathartic because it finalised death. But was death any more acceptable when one acknowledged its finality?

CHAPTER FOURTEEN

They entered Ifor Road from the north end so that the going was relatively level up to Ankover Lodge. They parked immediately in front of the house, then walked on until they could look down towards the corner. Noyes said: 'It's steep, all right.'

'And gets steeper nearer the corner,' Park said.

'I remember. OK, let's go back.'

They returned to Ankover Lodge and went up the stone path to the portico. When Gregg opened the door, Noyes formally expressed their condolences and apologies for bothering him at such a time, explained that there were some questions which had to be asked.

They went into the drawing room. Noyes, who knew enough about antiques normally to be able to judge the good from the ordinary,

126

was impressed by the quality of the contents.

He spoke briskly, but his manner remained friendly and it would have needed more astuteness than Gregg was able to summon at that time to realise the deviousness behind the words. 'I'm afraid we've learned something very disturbing and as a consequence I decided it should be me who told you what that is. The brakes of your car failed, which is why your wife suffered the tragic crash; it appears that they had been tampered with in a way that made certain they would fail under heavy braking.'

'Impossible!'

'Why?'

'You're suggesting someone wanted to kill Diana.'

'Or you, since normally you drove the Ford.'

'You mean . . .' Gregg was silent for a while, then he said harshly: 'It's because of the trial?'

'That seems probable, but we do have to investigate the possibility of someone else having a motive either to kill your wife or you. That's why we're here now.'

'She . . . she said over and over again I should have kept quiet about the threats, that my duty was first and foremost to make certain nothing happened to us. But I thought my duty was . . . How can one know what's right?'

'If I knew the answer, I'd be either a very lucky or a very clever man. Have you received any threats beyond those you've told us about?'

'No.'

'Nothing's happened that, looking back on it, could be interpreted as a threat?'

'No.'

'Was your wife ever threatened?'

'No.'

'Can you be certain of that?'

'She'd have told me if anything had happened because it would have ... have frightened her even more.'

'Can you think of anyone unconnected with the trial who might hate you or your wife so much that he'd wish to kill one of you?'

'Of course not.'

'Why d'you say, "of course not"?'

'Because the people we know would no more murder than fly.'

'That expression's rather out of date,' Noyes observed mildly. 'People do fly, all the time.'

'Most expressions eventually become meaningless in a literal sense, but figuratively remain expressive.'

'Of course. I'm afraid I've rashly ventured into your territory ... Then you can think of no one who might have cause, or even reckon he'd cause, to murder either you or your wife?'

'Apart from the men who did threaten me, no.'

'Then it seems we must assume that they, or someone behind them, were responsible for sabotaging the brake lines of the Ford. It also means that you were the target, not your wife. Why exactly was she driving your car?'

'She'd arranged to have coffee with a friend, but had forgotten she was having her car serviced. When I told her I was going into Shinstone, she suggested we swapped cars . . . I can't stop thinking that if I'd been driving the Ford, there might not have been so terrible an accident.'

'Why's that?'

'My wife drove quickly and was used to a car with first-class brakes; the Ford was roadworthy, but needed to be driven with sympathetic care. She must have gone down the hill far too quickly; I always go down slowly, in a low gear; perhaps the brakes wouldn't have failed for me. If they had failed, perhaps I'd have been able to avoid the barrier. So if only we hadn't swapped cars . . . If only. The two most useless words in the language.'

'Have you any idea why she wasn't wearing the seat belt?'

'She never did. She was terrified of being trapped in a fire.'

'Did she have medical exemption?'

'She wouldn't apply for that.'

'Why not?'

'She was reluctant to admit her fears, even to a doctor.'

'You didn't think to remind her, before you left, about driving carefully in your car?'

'I forgot to; as simple as that. Yet another *If only* . . . The ancient Greeks, as always, were far more realistic about life than we are. "Even God cannot change the past."'

'When you drive away from here, do you normally go downhill?'

'Yes. That's the quickest route to the centre of town.'

'Where does the friend of your wife live who she was going to have coffee with?'

'Close to the centre.'

'Then your wife would probably not have considered going the other way from here?'

'No.'

'Over the past couple of weeks, have you noticed a parked car you didn't recognise as belonging to someone who lives along the road?'

'I haven't, but I doubt I would have done unless it was something special like an Aston that would catch my attention.'

'I don't suppose vans are parked around here very often, but have you seen one?'

'No. Why d'you ask?'

'Because if you were the potential victim, the would-be murderer must have set out to gain an idea of your routine in order to formulate a plan.'

'Someone has kept this house under observation?'

'It seems possible . . . That about covers everything except to get from you the names and addresses of the people who work for you. We'll be asking them if they noticed anyone or any vehicle hanging around the place.'

'There's only Mrs Mabey and Althorpe. I can never remember his address, but it's in the library so I'll get it.'

Gregg left. Noyes stood, crossed to the smaller carpet, lifted one corner and folded it back to examine the underneath. He noticed the expression of curiosity on Park's face. 'Just confirming it's what it looks.' He replaced the corner, stood, dusted his hands. 'Very nice.' He sat.

Park said, in stilted tones: 'I read the other day that these sort of carpets are often made by child labour because their fingers are so nimble. They're sold into what's really slavery, get lousy food, work all hours, are beaten regularly, and raped when the boss is feeling frisky.'

'Could be.'

'Rather takes the shine off the carpets.'

'That's to mix emotion with fact. Whatever the living conditions of the people who made that carpet, they produced a beautiful piece of work.'

Park hoped his reaction to the sentiment expressed was not obvious. For him, not even a miracle of ancient art could be beautiful if the making of it had been at the cost of human suffering.

Gregg returned and handed a piece of paper

131

to Noyes. 'The two names and addresses.'

They said goodbye and left. Noyes settled behind the wheel of the CID Rover, started the engine.

'Don't forget the belt, sir,' Park said.

'Bloody thing.' Noyes clipped the belt home. He drew out from the pavement and accelerated carefully. They approached the corner. 'This is a right royal bastard. Even Nuvolari wouldn't have taken it at full chat.'

'Who's that?'

'Can you really be so ignorant?'

'Looks like it.'

'Nuvolari,' Noyes said, as he braked and began to turn into the hairpin bend, 'was arguably the greatest driver of all time. Stick him in a pedal car and he'd have it motoring like an Auto Union. Ask me what that was and you walk back to the station.'

They rounded the bend, continued down what was now Adeane Road to arrive at the T-junction. 'What's your verdict?' Noyes asked as he braked to a halt, checked left.

'I'd prefer not to buy a second-hand car from you, sir.'

He appeared to accept that as a compliment. 'Did you notice the papers on the table in the hall?' He drew out as the road cleared.

'*Mail* and *Times*.'

'Find out if the article Duggan remembers appeared in either of them.'

'That could be a very long job . . .'

'Then don't waste time getting it started. What do you make of Gregg?'

'More than a touch of the old school. Which is strange, seeing he's an author.'

'Proves they're not all long-haired, coke-snorting queers . . . What's your definition of "old school"? Looks the other way when a woman in a short skirt climbs over a stile?'

'Something like that.'

'You're a romantic . . . Let's get realistic. What can happen when a poor husband can't afford to buy his rich wife that little Gucci number she so likes? She starts looking at him with dissatisfaction, he becomes resentful and seeks solace with a bimbo who's willing to agree that his wife doesn't understand him. At which point, he realises that if he had his wife's money, but not her, life would be one long high.

'It's all beginning to make sense; all those inconsistencies are beginning to disappear.' Lights changed to red and they stopped. 'He's an active imagination or he wouldn't write books. So when he learned he was to be on jury duty, he dreamed up a scheme which would make his life happy. He'd say he'd had a threatening telephone call trying to make him sway the verdict. After a bit, he'd report a second one, more threatening than the first. There wasn't a third one because we'd had a caller identity unit installed on his line and told him that BT would be picking up any call that the unit couldn't identify. Instead, remembering how we'd warned him that the pressure might be increased, he strangled the dog.'

'You really think he could have?'

The lights went green and Noyes drove on. 'Is there anything a man won't do to grab a pot of gold?'

'I just can't see him doing anything so difficult emotionally and so brutal physically.'

'Murdering a dog's more difficult that murdering a wife? And aren't you forgetting the lack of footprints in the garden and the noose which was cut from a coil of wire in the shed? . . . He waited a few days after the trial was over, then set the final part of the plan in operation. The article in the paper had told him how to sabotage his own car; he knew his wife had fixed to take the Mercedes for service on the Monday; he told her he'd take her car and she could use his, certain she'd drive it far too quickly which would mean she'd have to brake like hell for the corner and that would fracture the brake lines. Afterwards, everyone would assume it was just an unfortunate accident. Ingenious. But as a literary type, he should have remembered that "There's many a slip 'twixt cup and lip". You'll have identified this slip?'

Park's mind had stayed with the problem which he saw as being presented by the picture of Gregg's taking the dog, which he had fed and petted for many years, tying a noose around its neck, and watching the scrabbling legs, the bulging eyes, the gaping jaws . . .

'To ensure that there cannot be a verdict of guilty, at least three members of the jury have to be suborned. All eleven others have twice been questioned and not one of them received any threats.'

'Perhaps it was thought that as foreman he'd be able to swing at least another two.'

'An operation like this would only be set up by a smart villain; smart villains know that the average juryman is as unpredictable as a whore's old age.' He turned right, into a road that would take them down to divisional HQ. 'So now we start finding I'm right.'

It was typical of Noyes, Park thought, not to have said 'if'.

CHAPTER FIFTEEN

Mrs Mabey opened the front door of her terraced house. A real tough 'un, Menzies judged. 'Local CID. D'you think I could have a word?'

'On a Sunday?'

'That's what I said to my sergeant, but he just told me to get on and do some work for a change.' He smiled, hoping she would find his

135

smile as appealing as did other women.

She obviously did not. She continued to stand squarely in the doorway. 'What about?'

'It would be easier to tell you inside.'

After considering the matter, she finally moved. He entered a passage, on the right-hand wall of which was a framed poster of the Southern Alps in New Zealand.

'Who is it?' a man called out from the room immediately to the right.

'A copper.'

There were sounds of movement and then a man, no taller than Menzies, but with much broader shoulders and a face that would have done credit to a retired bare-knuckle pugilist, appeared. 'So what's all this about, mate?' he demanded aggressively. 'What are you on about?'

'I need to ask your wife if she noticed any strange vehicles in Ifor Road over the last fortnight.'

'It's because of the crash?' Mrs Mabey asked.

'That's right.'

'When I heard . . .' She became silent.

'It's no good getting in a state over the likes of them,' muttered her husband.

'That's the kind of thing you would say.' She turned to Menzies. 'Best go in there, if Fred's not made too much of a mess.'

Only a Sunday newspaper, its several parts strewn across one of the armchairs, upset the

136

tidiness. She collected it up and put it on a stool. Menzies sat and studied four framed prints, on the opposite wall, that depicted country scenes which, while in no way obviously alien, seemed to him not to be in Britain.

'New Zealand,' she said, as if answering the unasked question. 'Our girl's there, married.'

Working on the principle that the quickest way of establishing a rapport was to talk about another's interests, Menzies told her he'd always wanted to go to New Zealand because he'd heard it was such a wonderful country. She told him that four years before, her daughter and son-in-law had paid for them to go out there and they'd had the most wonderful time of their lives. She went on to describe the people and the country in such vivid terms that Menzies hastily reassessed his initial opinion of her. She might look as sour as an unripe lime, might have spoken sharply to her husband, but these were poor guides to her true character.

He brought the subject of conversation round to parked cars in Ifor Road.

She shook her head. 'Didn't notice none; not that wasn't usually about.'

'Was there anyone hanging around the place?'

'No. What are you on about?'

'There's a bit of a problem about the accident that we've got to try to clear up,' he

137

said dismissively. 'But it doesn't look right now as if we're going to succeed. It can happen that way . . . All very tragic, isn't it?'

'It's that, all right.' She glared at her husband, challenging him to repeat what he'd said before.

'It seems she was driving too fast.'

'Wouldn't be the first time.'

'Is that so?'

'I've seen her start off like she never could slow for the corner. Daft.'

'Mr Gregg was telling us how he was always trying to persuade her not to drive so fast.'

'He would.'

'A thoughtful kind of bloke?'

'A sight more thoughtful than . . .' She stopped.

'Maybe you were going to say, than she was?'

'They was different,' she said equivocally.

'He seems really cut up.'

'What d'you expect?'

'It's a terrible shock however people have been getting on together. And if the truth's told, there are always a few rows, aren't there?'

'Are there?'

'Even the Greggs must have had one or two in their time?'

'I wouldn't know.'

'Never heard 'em going on at each other, then?'

'If I had, I wouldn't be telling you,' she

138

snapped.

'Why not?'

'Because it ain't any of your business.'

'You know something? The way you've just put things, you've got me thinking that maybe you did hear a good old row from time to time but don't like to say so now she's dead.'

'Then you can think different. I've too much work to do, thanks to a husband what thinks Sunday is a day of rest, to go on like this. So you can go and leave me to get on with it.'

'Fair enough.' Menzies thought that she and her husband probably had many a good old row.

*   *   *

Althorpe's younger son said his father was likely in the Black Swan. Duggan drove to the pub, went in, and asked if anyone knew where Althorpe was. He was directed to the man— who could have indicated who he was, but had chosen not to—who stood at the far end of the bar, an empty glass in front of him. He listened to Duggan, stared hard at his glass; when this had been refilled and Duggan had been handed a half of bitter, he led the way out to the garden at the back in which were three patio tables and chairs.

Duggan sat, raised his glass. 'First today and all the sweeter for it.'

Althorpe drank. The sunshine was sharp

139

and highlighted the lined roughness of his facial skin which marked him as a man who spent much of his time in the open.

Duggan put his glass down. 'It's like this. We're trying to clear up one or two problems that have arisen over the crash and thought that you may be able to help us.'

Althorpe offered no comment.

Because his character was in many ways not dissimilar to the other's, Duggan suffered no sense of annoyance in the face of such taciturnity. 'One of the things we need to know is whether in the days before the crash you saw a stranger hanging around Ankover Lodge; someone with nothing to do and all the time in the world to do it.'

Althorpe shook his head.

'If there had been, d'you reckon you'd have noticed?'

'If I was looking.'

'You work there during the week so wouldn't you have been looking?'

'Spend most of me time in the back. With the vegetables when she's not on about something else.'

'You can't see the road from there?'

'With the house and walls in the way?'

'When you've been working in the front garden, has there been a van or car parked in the road you've not seen before?'

'No.'

'Then it looks like maybe no one's been

hanging around the place.'

'Why should anyone?'

'It's a possibility we've had to check out.' He drank. He leaned back in the chair. 'Does a man good to feel the sun on him.' His relaxed manner suggested his work had been completed and now he was relaxing; he might lack imaginative initiative, but he possessed a strong degree of slyness. 'I suppose you've been in gardening a long time?'

'All me working life.'

'You know what you're doing, then.'

'I'd be a bloody fool if I didn't.'

'A mate of mine who's been to Ankover Lodge says the garden's a real treat. I hope the boss is grateful for all the hard work you do?'

'Her? Always more complaints than thanks.'

'She was the boss in the garden, not him?'

'And it wasn't just the garden,'

'You're saying she wore the trousers?'

'She'd the money.'

'That must have made things difficult for him at times?'

'Like as not.'

'I suppose she let him know who held the purse strings?'

'She'd a tongue, right enough.'

'You heard her going for him?'

'Them what are rich don't reckon the likes of me can hear.'

'So you've been in the garden working and they've been inside with a window wide open, having a row?'

'Aye.'

'Often?'

'Often enough.'

'What have they rowed over?'

'Lots of things.'

'Money?'

'She was forever telling him it was her what had to pay for the running of the place when it should be him.'

'That'll have annoyed him more than somewhat. I suppose he turned round and told her what he thought in no uncertain terms?'

'No.'

'No?'

'He ain't the kind to foul-mouth his wife.'

Duggan was surprised. He would have described himself as even-tempered, but if his wife had ever set out to make him feel small, he'd have had a lot to say. He drank, wiped his mouth with the back of his hand. 'Did you ever hear him threaten his wife?'

'You think a man like him would do that?' Althorpe said, contemptuous of such stupidity.

*　　　*　　　*

Gregg finally gave up his attempt to work and left the library. He was surprised to find Mrs Mabey was in the kitchen. 'You're still here? It's twenty minutes after your finishing time.'

'I reckoned you needed some grub. When a

142

man's on his own, he often don't bother to cook for himself.'

'But if you're not at home in time, your husband will miss his lunch.'

'He's not coming back today, so took his grub with him. I've peeled potatoes and sliced some runner beans and they're cooking; there's pork chops in the grill and all you have to do is turn on.'

'You are wonderfully kind.'

'Not doing any more than another would,' she said gruffly, embarrassed by the warmth in his words.

'I'm going to have a drink—will you join me?'

'If you say.'

'What would you like; gin, whisky, brandy, vodka, rum . . .'

'A bit of brandy and soda would do me a treat.'

He went through to the larder and poured out the drinks. Back in the kitchen, he handed her a glass. 'There's something I want you to know. Right now, I can't say what the future will be. But I'd be grateful if you'd stay until I can be certain what I'm going to do.'

'Don't you worry, Mr G. I'll be here until you don't need me no more.'

He looked at her and saw a woman whose appearance cruelly mocked her nature. He drained his glass. 'Let me get you the other half?'

'Not for me. Two of these and you'll have me doing "Knees up Mother Brown".'

'One day I'll tempt you into a second one for that pleasure!' He left to refill his glass. When he returned, she had just switched on the grill.

'There you are. All you have to do now is watch the chops for how you like 'em. There's apple sauce in the cupboard, there. Don't know what you want for pud, but there's ice cream in the deep-freeze.' She put her glass down. 'I had a caller yesterday morning. A detective. Asked if I'd seen anyone hanging around here or a strange car or van parked. D'you know why they're asking?'

'They told me that my Ford crashed at the corner because someone tampered with the brakes to make certain they failed.'

'You mean, it was deliberate?'

'Apparently.'

She was silent for a while, then said: 'But who'd want to do such a thing?'

'You must have seen on the telly that in the trial one of the jury was threatened if he didn't make certain the verdict wasn't guilty?'

She nodded.

'I was the person who was threatened. Consequently, the police think that whoever was behind the threats tried to get his own back on me for the guilty verdict. It was my wife's terrible misfortune to have ... to have been driving my car instead of me.'

She fingered a large mole on the right-hand side of her neck. 'The detective was trying to ask other questions.'

'Such as?'

'About you and Mrs Gregg. Whether you had rows.'

'What did you say to that?'

'Told 'em it was none of their business what goes on between a man and his wife.'

She told him that the potatoes were in the left-hand saucepan and the beans in the right-hand one—apparently not placing any faith in his ability to distinguish between the two—and to keep an eye on the chops; she'd be in smartly the next day and if he decided what he'd like for a meal and bought it, she'd either get it ready for cooking, or cook it. She left.

He checked the chops, decided they needed turning. As he drank, he wondered why the police had asked if he and Diana had rowed. Probably it had become second nature to them to pry into private lives even when any information gained could be of no consequence. His thoughts wandered and suddenly he suffered a feeling of loss that was not connected with Diana . . . Joe. Whenever meat had been cooking, she had appeared, drooling, goggling eyes appealing. He felt ashamed at this transfer of his grief, even though it had been beyond his will.

CHAPTER SIXTEEN

Noyes swore as he drove into the car park to find every space taken. Recognising one of the DC's cars, he double-parked in front of that, shamelessly exploiting his rank. He walked across to the entrance to the main building to meet Park, who was coming out. 'Any alarms?'

'There's nothing new that's urgent, but . . .' Park began.

'Right. I'll be off again as soon as I've collected the latest info that county are shouting for. Those bastards spend their lives working out how to waste other people's time.' He went to move past Park.

'There are two reports on the Gregg case you need to know . . .'

'Then give them to me, double quick.'

'Jim had a word with Mrs Mabey. She wasn't saying so, but he gained the impression that the Greggs had pretty frequent rows.'

'Did he explain how he gained an impression when she wasn't saying?'

'From the way in which she didn't say it.'

'I didn't know you'd Irish blood in you. What's the second report?'

'Mike questioned Althorpe who said he'd heard the Greggs having several rows, most times over money.'

'That makes sense. There's nothing going to

fire up a husband more than a rich wife who rams it down his throat that she does the paying.'

'As a matter of fact, we don't yet know for sure that he really is all that hard up . . .'

'Then you've not been doing your job. Find out.'

'Yes, sir,' said Park, phlegmatically accepting the unjust criticism. 'Althorpe told Mike something else. When she went for him all ends up, he just remained calm.'

'Beggars can't be critics.'

'I reckon that says he's not a man who'll ever go for a woman, not even his wife.'

'Are you on to that tack again? God Almighty, next thing you'll be telling me he's a verray parfit gentil knight. Have you traced which newspaper the article on defective brakes appeared in?'

'Steve's on that, but it's going to be a long job . . .'

'It won't be if he pulls his finger out. Has the Mercedes garage said when the car was booked in for its service?'

'I was about to get on to A Division and ask someone there . . .'

'The road to early retirement is paved with "abouts". Do it now.' Noyes went into the building. Park, deeming it advisable to delay what he had been going to do, followed at a slower pace.

*   *   *

147

Hamilton, a CID aide in A Division, which was centred on Shinstone, walked down High Street to the Mercedes showrooms, fronting a modern concrete and glass building. He stared at the blood-red 500SL and saw himself behind the steering wheel, drawing up in front of 64 Ascor Road, and suggesting to Janet that they went for a spin. If that didn't work the trick, nothing short of a walk up the aisle would . . .

He went in and spoke to a very superior blonde receptionist and then, in the garage behind the showrooms, to a middle-aged man in an oil-stained boiler suit whose accent was local and was his kind of person.

They went into a glass-walled, cluttered office in which a young woman was working at the smaller desk.

'It's local CID wanting some information, Heather. See if you can give it to them.' The foreman turned to Hamilton. 'Let me know if there's anything more we can do for you.'

'Cheers, mate.'

The foreman left. She said: 'So what is it you want?'

'Did Mrs Gregg's car come in for servicing recently?'

She tapped out instructions on the keyboard of the PC and information appeared on the monitor. 'Is that Mrs J. Gregg, Ankover Lodge, Ifor Road, Addington?'

'She's the one.'

'We do her car regular.'

'So was it in here on the nineteenth of this month?'

She tapped out more instructions and fresh information appeared on screen. 'Yeah.'

'Would she have rung you first thing that morning to ask you to do it?'

'No way. Services have to be booked in advance; sometimes, as much as two or three weeks.'

'Then she'll have booked in on the fifth, or earlier?'

'Hang on and I'll see. It's all down here . . . The booking was made on the second.'

'Would you know who made it?'

'She'll have done that, won't she?'

'You can't say if it was her or someone else doing it for her?'

'No can do.'

Hamilton noted down the date. As he closed the notebook, he wondered what case was involved. Requests for information from other divisions or forces were often irritating because one seldom learned the reason for, or the result of, one's work.

*   *   *

Noyes, who had been standing by the window in his office, his mind not on what he saw, turned as Park entered.

'Steve's just been on the blower, sir. The

149

article and the accompanying diagram showing how the brake lines of the Escort were sabotaged appeared in the *Daily Mail* on the twenty-fourth of April.'

Noyes returned to the chair behind the desk. 'So now we can be certain he had the opportunity to know what to do and how to do it.'

'Another thing. A Division has come through to say that Mrs Gregg's Merc was booked in for service on the second of the month.'

'Who booked it in?'

'They couldn't tell us.'

'Pity. Still, I reckon we can begin to fill in some of the details.' He leaned further back in the chair, stared at a point on the far wall. 'She mentions her car's coming up to needing a service, he says he'll get on to the garage, knowing near enough the times he has to work to. After the trial's started, he feeds us the story that he's received a threatening telephone call. Three days later, he tells us he's had a second one and this time it was made by a foreigner—supposedly, we're likely to be doubly impressed by the thought of a dastardly foreigner trying to suborn an honest Englishman. We arrange for a caller identification unit to be installed and tell him that if that's by-passed, the exchange will still nail the source. That means he can't report a third call, maybe made by Dracula. But we'd also advised him that while the villains would never actually carry out their specific threat, they'd do all they could to increase the pressure and this gives him the idea of strangling the dog. Are you with me?'

'Up to a point.'

'What point?'

'I just can't believe he would strangle the dog.'

'Why not?'

'Because—'

Noyes interrupted him. 'Tell me he has too noble a character and I'll have you pounding the beat on the night turn.'

Park mentally shrugged his shoulders.

'The trial finished and everything's ready for lift-off. He fixes the brakes of his own car on the Sunday, on the Monday morning tells her he has to go into Shinstone so wouldn't it be a good idea if he took her car for its service and she used his to have coffee with a friend. After he's left, she drives off in the Ford, heading downhill too fast and not wearing the belt, leaves the braking so late she has to slam them on with every ounce of force and the weakened lines rupture. The car hits the barrier at an angle, somersaults, and ends up down in a garden with her dead. Seemingly, everything's worked like clockwork. Only he's overlooked the fact that every vehicle involved in a fatal is examined to try to find the cause of the crash. Now how do you read it?'

'Everything does seem to fit, but . . .'

'You've more buts than a herd of billy goats.'

'You do have to admit that his version of events fits the facts equally well.'

'Which is why we're going to take everything apart to confirm mine is correct.'

CHAPTER SEVENTEEN

Bell, an editor at Alan Cresswell Ltd., whose offices had moved out of central London several years before, had the air of a pedant, thanks to a very high forehead and a sometimes over-careful way of talking. He rested his elbows on the desk—which had on it a couple of manuscripts, a set of galley proofs, several books, and a note from his wife reminding him to buy a present for their younger daughter—and joined the tips of his fingers together, looking at the detective constable over the triangle so formed. 'It's an unusual request. And you lack the authority to demand I disclose the figures, do you not?'

'I've no warrant, sure, but . . .' Snow began.

'Then I will wait to give you the information until you can produce one.'

'Why, when it can't do any harm?'

'That must depend on one's point of view. From yours, I'm sure you are correct; from Mr Gregg's, the opposite holds good. He would be the first to say that a man's income is his private affair unless and until it becomes absolutely necessary for it to be disclosed.'

'So I'm here to say it's become absolutely necessary.'

'On what grounds?'

'In connection with the death of his wife.'

'My God! Are you telling me she's died? How? When?'

'There was a road accident a few days back.'

'I must give him my very sincere commiserations. So relatively young! Truly, in the midst of life we are in death.'

'About the details of his sales . . .'

'How can they be of the slightest significance in connection with this most unfortunate accident?'

'I couldn't say.'

'Then I feel under even less necessity to give them to you.'

'It would save our having to take the matter further.'

'I prefer to concentrate on saving myself trouble, not other people.'

Ever more bleeding pompous, Snow thought antagonistically. 'Not very successful, is he? I've never heard of him.'

'Is that the criterion by which his work should be judged?'

Snow's irritation became more apparent. 'I read a lot.'

'I was not trying to suggest you did not.

Merely that, sadly, the worth of a book in these days is so often assessed solely by its sales. Not being a film star, a sleazy politician, or a toe-sucked ex-royal, Mr Gregg is not famous or infamous in his own right and his only asset as an author is his ability to use words to explore the common predicaments of all humanity.'

'Which, boiled down, means he doesn't sell?'

'All I am implying is that his books deserve greater success than an unknowledgeable public is prepared to accord them. As a publisher, it distresses me that when it comes to sales, hype has superseded ability.'

'How many books a year does he write? Or is that also a state secret?'

'I suppose on average, one.'

'Not so long ago there was a bit in the paper saying the average book didn't make enough to keep a family of one above the poverty line.'

'Newspapers thrive on clichés with the consequence that artists, composers, and authors live either in mansions or garrets.'

'I can't think why anyone bothers to write books,' Snow said as he stood.

'There are many who regard the craft as a sign of incipient insanity.'

*　　　*　　　*

After a brisk walk along the rides through Park Wood, Gregg returned to the Mercedes.

154

Exercise was proving to be a way in which he could temporarily keep the black clouds at bay. He drove out of the lay-by and, choosing a circular route through Addington, approached Ifor Road from the top end, thereby avoiding the twisted Armco barrier, not yet replaced, which still marked the spot where Diana had crashed.

He parked in front of the garage, locked the car, and then stood and stared at it. Should he get rid of it because it had been hers and therefore carried memories? Should he keep it, because it gave him such pleasure to drive that those memories were softened until it was almost as if she had left him a farewell gift? . . .

He turned and walked along the stone path towards the house. He was now not in two minds about what he'd do with that. He'd put it up for sale as soon as he was legally entitled to do so. Then he'd buy a place in the country, surrounded by its own land, preferably with only fields, hedges, and woods in sight; centuries old, slightly crooked walls, a peg-tile roof, oak beams, at least one inglenook fireplace, and maybe even a priest's hole. A home, not a declaration of wealth.

Mrs Mabey had prepared his lunch which, as she informed him, was roast beef, baked potatoes, and peas.

'And there was a telephone for you earlier. He said he'll ring again.' She vigorously dried some cooking dishes she had just washed.

'Did he say who he was?'

'I don't remember the name, but it's down on the pad.'

He returned to the hall and read the name. Bell. Script queries were usually put by his assistant, so this call could be in respect of something important. Film, television, even radio rights . . . He dialled the number, very conscious of the tension of expectation. When the call was through, he said: 'It's John Gregg. I gather you rang?'

'I wanted to tell you that I've only just heard the tragic news. I am so terribly sorry.'

Shamingly, he felt this to be an anticlimax.

'I know this is one time when words are almost useless . . .'

He listened and thanked the other at appropriate moments.

'Just before I ring off, I thought you should know I've had the police here, asking some very impertinent questions which concerned you.'

'What did they want to know?'

'Basically, how much money you made at writing.'

'What did you tell them?'

'That the matter is confidential.'

'Did they explain why they were asking?'

'The young man said little more than that it was because of the tragic death of Diana. I still fail utterly to understand how the information he sought could be in any way germane.'

156

'It sounds ridiculous.'

'I agree. It might well be in your interests to raise the matter with the competent authority.'

'Perhaps I will.'

'Spurious authority is the curse of our age ... If there is any way in which I can help in this sad time, please don't hesitate to let me know.'

'Thanks.'

Gregg said goodbye, replaced the receiver. Bell had expected, but not received, an explanation; he hadn't given one because he could not do so. He would have thought there was not a single member in the police force who gave a damn whether he sold a thousand or a hundred thousand copies of each book.

Mrs Mabey came into the hall, handbag in one hand, a plastic mackintosh—even though the day was fine—in the other. 'Everything's going along fine, Mr G, so all you'll have to do is dish up in twenty minutes. There's apple pie and a pot of cream in the refrigerator for afters.'

'That's great.'

'Been meaning to tell you. The old man was saying what happened on Sunday.'

It amused him that she usually referred to Althorpe as 'the old man'. At a guess, there was no more than five years' difference between their ages.

'He was in the pub when a detective turned up. Asked a lot of questions, mostly about you and Mrs G.'

'What kind of questions?'

'Whether you and her maybe sometimes didn't get on too well together. I told him he was an old fool for answering.'

'What did he tell them?'

'That he'd heard you and her having a bit of a barney now and then. Who doesn't? I'll bet his Maggie tells him what's what when he talks more stupid than usual . . . Just thought you ought to know.'

'It's kind of you to tell me.'

'I'll be on my way, then.' She left.

Had she not spoken to him so soon after the telephone call from Bell, he would—because his mind was so confused—probably have held the information to be irrelevant, ignoring the fact that two days before a detective had visited her house and questioned her. But when in such quick succession he learned that on two separate occasions the police had shown unusual interest in the relationship between Diana and himself, it was impossible to miss the inference. His instinct was to tell the detective inspector not to be such a fool; a more reasoned reaction was to accept that such a course of action might arouse further suspicion rather than allay that which already existed. Better to let the police poke and pry because then the sooner they'd realise the impossibility of his having had anything to do with Diana's death.

Noyes parked the car, looked through the windscreen at the small town house. 'All right, let's go and see what the mother-in-law thinks of things.'

It became very obvious, very quickly that Mrs Grantley believed in exposing her emotions. She detailed her grief in terms which initially embarrassed the two detectives, despite their experience, then began to irritate them. And after listening for the third time to a description of Diana's saintly virtues, Noyes steered the subject of the conversation around to Gregg. 'He is, of course, very badly shocked.'

'Perhaps,' she said, biting the word short. Her expression tightened, making her look old and crabby.

'You surely don't think . . .' He didn't finish.

'You know why he married my daughter?'

'I imagine for the usual reason.'

'For her money.'

'Isn't that being a little unkind?'

'When she said she was going to marry him, I told her not to be so silly when she ought to be doing so much better for herself.'

'But she wouldn't listen to you?'

'Tried to tell me that her money meant nothing to him and in any case, soon he'd be earning a fortune because he'd become so successful. Successful? When he's too lazy to get a proper job? Who had to buy the house? Who had to pay for the running of it? She did. Who bought her car? She did.'

'That could have disturbed her less than you think. She might have been so proud of his writing that she was glad to help him financially.'

'You wouldn't say that if you knew what life was like for her recently.'

'What was wrong with it?'

'She never had any fun because he did everything he could to spoil things.'

'That sounds a bit . . . Well . . .'

'I'm her mother, aren't I? I could tell from being with her—she didn't have to say anything. Things were so bad, she needed a holiday and wanted to go to the West Indies. She offered to pay for the both of them, but he wouldn't go because he knew she wanted him to be with her.'

'You don't think it might have been his pride which made him refuse?'

'How can he have any pride when he's such a failure? It was spite, that's what it was. Have you met him?'

'Yes, we have.'

'And you're detectives, but can't tell the kind of man he is. If you listened to Carol, you'd soon learn.'

'Who's Carol?'

'My other daughter. She knew him for what he is the moment she met him.'

'I reckon it might be an idea to have a chat with her so I'll ask you for her address before we leave . . . Mrs Grantley, there is something you should know. An examination of the car in which your daughter so tragically died showed that the brake lines had been tampered with.'

'You mean it was deliberate?'

'I'm afraid so.'

'He murdered her,' she screamed.

'I know it makes everything even more tragic for you, but you really shouldn't make such an accusation without reason. Unless you know as fact Mr Gregg might well have been involved in your daughter's death, it will be much better for everyone if you say nothing.'

'Or course it was him.'

'To your knowledge, did he ever threaten her?'

'All the time.'

'You know that of your own knowledge?'

She said wildly: 'Diana told me he was always threatening her, saying he'd get rid of her so he could have her money. Arrest him.'

'If we find we have cause to do so, we will.' Noyes stood. 'Perhaps you'll be kind enough to give us your daughter's address?'

She managed to calm down sufficiently to give this to them. Noyes listened with strained patience to a further demand that they arrest Gregg, then led the way out of the house.

As he sat in the car and clipped home the seat belt, he said: 'What would you do if you had her as a mother-in-law?'

'Either cut her throat or my own,' Park replied.

'How much of what she said do we believe?'

'As much as you could write on the head of a pin in capital letters.'

'It just might not all be lies.'

'I suppose she could have a daughter called Carol . . . Guv, there was no mention of threats until you asked about 'em. If he really had threatened his wife, that old bitch would have tied her tongue in knots in her hurry to tell us as soon as we'd introduced ourselves.'

Noyes started the engine, backed, turned. 'Why d'you reckon she hates him so much?' he asked as he drove forward.

'From what she let drop, she reckoned her daughter ought to have married someone much higher up on the social ladder.'

'That would be a bloody stupid reason.'

'Life's full of 'em.'

CHAPTER EIGHTEEN

The Barnards lived on the outskirts of Ongar in a private estate of houses which had been carefully designed and set out to appear from the road to be larger and more luxurious than they were. Detective Constable Selby braked to a halt, visually checked the name on the wooden gate which needed painting, switched off the engine. He left the car and walked up the path to the porch, pressed the bell. The door was opened by a woman a shade older than he. 'Mrs Barnard?'

'Yes,' she answered, her tone sharp.

Vinegary, he thought. 'It's all right, I'm not selling encyclopaedias. I'm DC Selby, local CID.'

'Oh! I suppose it's about my sister?'

'That's right.'

'Come in, then.'

He entered a small hall and from there followed her into a sitting room that had been furnished for effect rather than comfort.

She sat. 'Was she murdered?'

'What makes you ask that?'

'My mother phoned me. I thought she was being hysterical, but you coming here makes me think maybe she wasn't. So what's the truth?'

He chose his words with care. 'It's not our investigation and we don't know all the details.'

'Were the brakes of the car deliberately damaged?'

'I can answer that one; yes, they were.'

'Then it was murder.'

'Not necessarily, Mrs Barnard, it could be a case of manslaughter; it all depends. That's why I'm hoping you'll be able to give us some facts.' He brought his notebook out of his pocket, together with a ballpoint pen. 'What I'd like to learn first is how you and your sister were—would you say the two of you were close?'

'How close is close? It's quite a long drive to Addington because the traffic's usually heavy and there's the tunnel to get through, so we didn't see each other all that much. But we were often on the phone for a chat.'

'When did you last speak to her?'

'We had a meal with them something like three weeks ago and I rang the next day to find out how she was.'

'What sort of evening was it at her house?'

'To begin with, all right. Then the dog was found strangled and she went all to pieces because she was so ridiculously fond of it. I once asked her why—she wouldn't answer. I reckon it was either because an old flame gave it to her or it offered her something she didn't get elsewhere.'

'What kind of something?'

'Pets can become substitutes for all sorts of things.'

'How exactly did she react to the dog's death?'

'By saying ridiculous things.'

'What sort of things?'

'Does it really matter?'

'I'm afraid it may do.'

'She blamed John—my brother-in-law—for the dog's death. Said it would never have

164

happened but for him. She even became so wild that at one point she told him to clear out of the house.'

He wrote quickly.

'Look, my sister didn't mean everything she was saying; I'm sure she couldn't have done.'

'Very understandable,' he said and continued writing.

'Just before we left, the doctor arrived and gave her something which calmed her right down and made her sleep. When I phoned the next morning, she was bitterly sad, of course, but not hysterical. Still blaming him, but . . .' She became silent.

'If I asked if your sister was happy, what would you say?'

'That with her money, she should have been.'

'But wasn't?'

'It's almost impossible to judge the quality of other people's lives, but I have wondered more than once if Mother was right and Di made a mistake when she married John. Their characters were so different; she wanted the fun of life, underneath his flippant manner he's serious about so many things. But before meeting him, she was very friendly with a man who suddenly married someone else and that left her shellshocked; when John turned up, he caught her on the rebound, apart from which, she thought it would be exciting to be married to an author. People in the art world are seldom modest about their potentials.'

'D'you think he's successful these days?'

'As he once said to me, define success. The critics seem to like his work—but then critics like to pose—the public doesn't. And having tried to read his stuff, I can't say I'm very surprised. The general public doesn't want to have to think hard to understand what a book's about.'

'Then in financial terms, he can't be very successful?'

'I imagine that's a tactful way of putting things.'

'But your sister was quite well off?'

'Rich is the word you're looking for.' Her tone had become bitter. 'Her godfather had no children and left her a fortune. My godfather left me a set of silver teaspoons which turned out to be plate.'

'Then it can't have mattered to Mr Gregg that he didn't make all that much?'

'If he'd been practical, it wouldn't have done. But I don't think he's ever been able to come to terms with the way things were because he felt humiliated every time she paid for something because he couldn't. Husbands don't like their wives to be very much better off than they are, do they?'

'I've never been lucky enough to find out . . . I suppose there were times when this situation caused trouble?'

'In what way?'

'Well, perhaps a row or two?'

'It would have been odd if not.'

'Did your sister ever talk to you about such rows?'

'She was far too loyal. But, of course, there are times when one . . .' She stopped.

'Yes?'

'Nothing.'

'Would you think Mr Gregg has a quick temper?'

'Whatever his emotions, he keeps them firmly under wraps. Even when he feels like blowing his top, he'll keep on smiling.'

'Your mother has said that on more than one occasion he threatened his wife.'

She was silent.

'Did your sister ever mention such an incident to you?'

'I need a cigarette. Do you smoke?'

'No, I don't.'

'Lucky you!' She left the room.

He wrote, using his own form of speedwriting and making copious notes so that he would be able to draw up a full and accurate record of the meeting when he was back at the station.

She returned, crossed to the window and stared out at the small back garden whose condition suggested that for the occupants gardening was a chore, not a pleasure.

'You were going to tell me, Mrs Barnard, if your sister ever mentioned to you that she had been threatened by her husband.'

'I was not.' She swung round. 'If something is said to me in confidence, I do not go around repeating it.'

'In other words, she did tell you she had?'

'In other words, I've no intention of answering you, one way or the other.'

'Don't you think you owe it to your sister's memory to make certain the truth is known?'

'Don't you think that that is being very sanctimonious?'

He flushed. 'This is a serious case and . . .'

'I don't give a damn. I was brought up to believe that loyalty is next to godliness.'

He accepted that she would not directly answer the question. He thought for a moment, then closed his notebook and returned it, and the pen, to his coat pocket. 'Thank you for your assistance at such a sad time.' He had seen people more clearly grief-stricken than she.

*   *   *

Noyes finished reading the fax, looked up at Park. 'It reads like DC Selby's swallowed a beginner's guide to popular psychology.'

'A youngster, trying to make his mark.'

'Still, with all that, a sight more informative than some of the reports your lads try to hand in.'

Park let that pass unchallenged.

'Cut out the possiblys, maybes, and I-think-it-likely-thats, and here's confirmation the marriage was rocky: he resented her wealth, they rowed, and he threatened her, probably quite frequently; confirmation, but not proof.'

'Even if the sister was ready to be completely forthcoming, the court would throw out a lot of her evidence as inadmissible because the last thing the law wants is to understand all the facts—'

Noyes interrupted him. 'Spare me. It's our job to work under the conditions as laid down and if the people laying them down are bloody fools, so be it . . . It's time to have another word with Gregg to find out what the estate's worth and if he's the main beneficiary. Tomorrow morning at ten. Tell him.'

'At his place or here?'

'His. He'll be more relaxed and we can keep it friendly if that seems to be the course to take.'

*   *   *

Barnard arrived home late. A few months previously there had been rumours of coming redundancies at work and since then he had been putting in considerable voluntary overtime in an attempt to suggest that others could be spared more readily than he. As he shut the front door, Carol came out of the sitting room into the hall. 'I was beginning to

169

get worried.'

'I thought I'd better finish what I was doing.'
He hung his lightweight mackintosh on the
hallstand.

'You look worn out.'

'That's how I feel.'

'Then you need a drink to buck you up.'
He was surprised since it was unusual for
her to suggest a homecoming drink. Because
she was virtually teetotal at home, drinking was
a waste of money, unlike a new frock or pair of
shoes . . .

'Has work been worse than usual?'

'Not really. But . . . The redundancies are
official now, though there's no word yet on the
numbers involved. People are talking about ten
per cent in the office as well as on the floor.'

'That leaves ninety per cent.'
He was surprised for the second time; he
would have expected her to treat the news with
deep pessimism since from the moment he'd
cautiously mentioned the possibility of
redundancies, she'd been frightened and
bitter; frightened that he'd be one of those
who suffered because she did not rate his
abilities highly, bitter because this would widen
still further the gulf that lay between her sister
and her.

'Get your drink and then I've something to
tell you.'
He went into the kitchen and over to the
cupboard in which were kept the few bottles,

poured out a good measure of whisky and then, since the bottle was only a quarter empty, a little more. He added water and ice, carried the glass through to the sitting room.

'Guess who called this morning,' she said as he sat.

'Joanna?'

'A detective.'

'Then your mother wasn't having hysterics when she phoned you!'

'He told me that the brakes of the car *had* been tampered with so it *wasn't* an accident and Di *was* murdered.'

'Jesus!' He drank. 'It hits below the belt when something like this happens so close to home.'

'Do you know who's suspect *numero uno*?'

'How could I?'

'John.'

'Try pulling the other one. John's the last person to kill anyone, let alone his wife.'

'You obviously think he's no more than the man he makes himself out to be—amusing, cool, kind?'

'Why not?'

'Because it's hardly an accurate picture if he killed Di.'

'That's putting the cart in front of the horse. If he didn't do it, it is an accurate picture. What makes you think he could possibly do such a terrible thing?'

'The money.'

'Married to her, he's always had the benefit of that.'

'Haven't you ever realised how proud he is? Try talking to him about his work and he either steers the conversation away from it or becomes facetious. Why? Because he's ashamed of his lack of any success. Look how he's always resented having to rely on her to foot the bills so that if he could get his own back, he did. When she wanted a holiday in Jamaica, or wherever it was, he wouldn't go. Why? Because she'd have had to pay for everything. His continuing humiliation must have built up until he decided to do something about it.'

'You ... you really can believe he killed her?'

She reached down for her handbag at the side of the chair and brought out of it a silver case. She lit a cigarette. 'The detective was quite a pleasant young man, rather serious when he wanted to know how Di and John got on together.'

'What did you say to that?'

'They were of very different characters.'

His tone became worried. 'If you put it that baldly, I hope it didn't give him the wrong impression. He could have thought you meant they didn't get on too well together.'

'He did ask if they had rows.'

'You told him, of course they didn't?'

'That would have been stupid. All couples

have rows.'

'Yes, but . . . Not the kind that lead to anything serious.'

'What happened when John told her he'd found the dog dead? She went for him all ends up.'

'Only because she was so potty about it. Surely you didn't mention that?'

'I had to, after he'd explained it was my duty to tell him the truth.'

'But . . .'

'Stop worrying. I didn't let on about everything. When he mentioned Mother had told the police John had threatened Di and he wanted to know if Di ever spoke to me about such threats, I told him that when something's said to me in the strictest confidence, I'll never reveal it to anyone.'

He stared at her, wondering how someone so sharp normally could have been so stupid.

'Why are you looking at me like that?'

'Don't you see that the way you spoke could have made him believe Di *had* told you that John had threatened her?'

She gave no answer.

He drained his glass, stood. 'I'm going to have another drink.' He expected a snide comment, but there was none. He left the room. When he returned, she was lighting another cigarette. 'I just hope to God the detective had the sense to realise you didn't mean it that way.' He sat.

She drew on the cigarette, exhaled. 'He seemed rather naïve.'

His voice rose. 'Are you saying he probably did think that?'

'What's it matter? The police don't suspect someone unless he's almost certainly guilty.'

'There must be one hell of a lot of people who'd argue with that proposition.'

'Only because they always criticise authority.'

'Is it because the police seem to suspect John that you told the detective what happened after he found the dead dog?'

'Are you saying it wasn't my duty to tell the detective the truth?'

He drank. Who held the moral high ground, she or he? He was certain he did, yet accepted that his certainly could not be justified.

*   *   *

He was reading a paperback in bed when she said: 'Have you stopped to think what will happen when John's found guilty of murdering Di?'

He turned his head to look at her in the other bed. 'Since I can't believe he had anything to do with her death, no, I haven't.'

'If Di's left him everything, he won't be able to have it because a convicted criminal isn't allowed to benefit from his crime. So it'll be as if she died intestate, which means her money

174

will go to Mother. And since Mother's getting very old, she doesn't need anything more than she's got—and in any case, she can't last much longer . . . It's not going to matter if they do make you redundant, is it?'

He tried to banish from his mind the questions before they were fully formed, but failed. When it appeared she had spoken stupidly to the detective, had she known precisely what she was doing? Had it not been a sense of duty to the truth which had made her reveal so much, had her prompt been jealousy and greed?

CHAPTER NINETEEN

As Gregg came out of the bedroom and walked to the landing, the long-case clock with shell-carved front struck the hour. He came to a stop and stared at it, remembering. Diana had bought it at a sale, in the face of several dealers who had failed to identify it as a Wheaton. It had been obvious that the pleasure it gave her had not been gained from its intrinsic beauty, or even its greatly increased value, but the knowledge that she had made a fool of several competitors. It had shown him an unattractive side to her character which he had not previously suspected. It had confirmed that to know thyself might be very difficult, to know someone else was impossible.

He continued on downstairs. He prepared breakfast and ate at the kitchen table. In little over an hour, the police would arrive to ask more questions—confirmation that their suspicions were still very active. Since they had made the move, he could rebut their absurd suspicions without arousing in their minds the thought that he who rushed to shout his innocence was trying to drown the whisper of his guilt. He felt more cheerful.

They arrived at two minutes after the hour. Both were dressed casually, Noyes a shade more smoothly than Park. He offered them coffee, which Noyes, without reference to Park, refused for both of them.

Once settled in the green room, Noyes said, in dismissive tones: 'Just a few questions to clear up one or two points. I think you've told us that you did not know your wife had booked her car in for a service at the Mercedes garage in Shinstone until the Monday on which she so sadly died?'

'That's right.'

'Would you know, in fact, when she made that booking?'

'No.'

'It was on the second of the month, seventeen days previously. She didn't tell you at the time?'

'Obviously not.'

'That seems a little odd since your wife would need to leave her car in town.'

'Why should it be odd?'

'I'd have thought she'd have checked with you if you could pick her up that day.'

'I can never be certain when I won't be working.'

'Are you saying that you didn't normally fetch her from Shinstone when she left her car there?'

'If I'm working, no. Either she stayed in town for the day, or she got a taxi back home.'

'And you would drive her in to collect the Mercedes when the service was finished?'

'The garage drove it out here and the driver returned in a second car.'

Park asked the next question. 'What newspapers do you regularly have, Mr Gregg?'

'*The Times* and the *Daily Mail*?.'

'Then you would have received the *Mail* on the twenty-fourth of April, this year?'

'I suppose so.'

'You don't remember?'

'I'm hardly likely to be able to be that specific.'

Noyes said: 'You might. That was the day when the paper reported that a husband had tried to murder his wife by tampering with the brake lines of her car and it showed a diagram which explained what he'd done.'

'Implying what?'

'No more than that you had the opportunity

177

to see this diagram.'

'Raising the further implication that if I'd seen it, I might have used the expertise to make certain my wife crashed when she borrowed the car?'

'We have to consider all possibilities.'

'However impossible?'

'After a few years in the police force, one realises that where people are concerned, nothing is impossible. How would you describe your relations with your wife?'

'Normal.'

'Despite the fact that circumstances were so unusual?'

'In what way?'

'I understand that she was a wealthy woman.'

'That she was better off than I, was not a fact I welcomed, but we'd both learned to accept the situation.'

'It didn't cause you a sense of resentment?'

Gregg hesitated. 'To tell the truth, there were moments when I regretted the fact.'

'At which time, you were resentful?'

'That's too strong a word.'

'Did this regret lead to you and your wife having rows?'

'Disagreements.'

'You choose your words very carefully.'

'To make certain you do not read into them what's not there.'

'Did some of your disagreements become

heated?'

'They did not. I like to pride myself that I'm sufficiently adult to be able to behave in a civilised manner.'

'Was your wife equally restrained?'

'Of course.'

'Then it's not true that she became hysterical when the dog was found dead in the garden and accused you of having killed it?'

'Not in the sense that I'd strangled Joe. Di always said I was stupid to report the threats, so when Joe was killed, she blamed me for being indirectly responsible.'

'The accusation must have upset you?'

'I could quite understand why she made it.'

'Then you must be a very understanding person.'

'Is that cause for sneering?'

'I'm not sneering. Just astonished by your forbearance . . . Do you know the contents of your wife's will?'

'Yes.'

'Who is her main beneficiary?'

'Is that any of your business?'

'Mr Gregg, there are mostly two ways of doing something; the pleasant and the unpleasant. You can tell us now and everything will be nice and quiet; or you can refuse so that we have to apply for an order to make you disclose the facts and inevitably the matter becomes public.'

After a while, Gregg said: 'I am the sole

179

beneficiary. When we made our wills, each of us left everything to the survivor.'

'In your wife's case, the estate will be considerable?'

'And conversely, had I died first, mine would not?'

'A possibility we are not called upon to consider,' Noyes said blandly. 'Roughly, how much will your wife's estate amount to?'

'I don't know.'

'You must have some idea.'

'I have never pried into my wife's financial affairs. On the contrary, I have refused to know anything about them.'

'From a sense of pride?'

'I suppose you could call it that if you wish.'

'Presumably, your wife had financial advisers?'

'Stockbrokers.'

'Their name?'

'Kelsey and Eyestone.'

'She must have received statements from them, including quarterly or monthly valuations of her holdings?'

'Yes. And to answer your next question, since she did not invite me to look at them, I have never done so.'

'Your lack of curiosity does you credit.'

'Only if you believe it normal to invade another's privacy without permission.'

'Apart from this house and her stocks and shares, did your wife have anything else of consequence?'

'The gallery.'

'What gallery is that?'

'Abbotts, in Shinstone.'

'I don't know it. Is it an art gallery?'

'Art and antiques.'

'She owned it?'

'Yes.'

'Does someone else run it?'

'She has a manager. She wasn't there much of the time, but she did all the main buying and kept a very close watch on the running. It was a hobby; but in some ways more than a hobby because . . . Life, as Lacton noted, turns no less confusingly than a country lane.'

'I don't follow that.'

'I was remembering . . . When my wife started work, she did so at Abbotts as an assistant/receptionist. The place exuded bogus taste and she was taken on because she had a suitable speaking voice. She soon discovered she'd a natural flair for the work and she developed this gift until she had a far better judgment than the owner; acknowledging this, he'd have sacked her if she hadn't become too valuable to the business. Then she inherited her godfather's estate and immediately chucked in the job, as a gesture of contempt, not because she'd become fed up with it. Soon after we were married, she read that the business had gone into liquidation and she bought it from the receiver and set about turning it into what she was certain it should always have been. She was very successful. She attended sales and often managed to buy something other dealers had missed or misattributed. If she'd given her whole energy to the business...' He stopped. 'I'm boring you.'

'Far from it.'

'Is there anything more you want to know?'

'The name of your wife's solicitors, for one thing.'

'Trumbell.'

'From Shinstone? A very old-fashioned firm; the kind who tend to dislike handling criminal cases.'

'Is that meant to be a pointed observation?'

'Merely a casual one.'

Gregg spoke challengingly. 'I hate violence in any shape or form and however much I disliked someone, I'd never use it; I did not strangle Joe; I did not sabotage the brakes of my car; I did not murder my wife. Why the hell won't you believe me?'

'Frankly, before we can do that without reservation, there are a couple of problems which have to be solved.'

'What are they?'

'We've learned nothing to suggest why anyone should have been so concerned that Lipman was not found guilty that when he was, you were targeted to be murdered in an act of frustrated revenge.

'Secondly, someone smart enough to set up the operation must be smart enough to have realised that even if you were foreman of the jury, on your own you couldn't guarantee to swing the jury, so at least two other members would have to be nobbled. We've twice questioned the other eleven and no attempt was made to suborn any of them.'

'Then two of them have to be lying.'

'That seems unlikely.'

'You've just said the opposite.'

'I said that at least two would have had to have been approached if a reasonable attempt to fix the verdict had been made. None of 'em have been.'

'I know I'm telling the truth, so unless someone else refused to knuckle down to the threats, the odds have to be that the two who voted not guilty are lying. Question them again.'

'We have no idea who they were.'

'Hendry and Akers. Make them admit the truth; force it out of them.'

'Aren't you the man who abhors all force? The rules governing the questioning of witnesses prohibits us from using any untoward pressure.'

'Rules are more important than uncovering the truth? Rules are more important than proving I didn't murder my wife?'

'Unless we become a police state, yes.'

'A shield to protect the incompetent.'

'To prevent barbarity.' Noyes stood. 'No doubt we'll need to ask you more questions at a later date.'

Manners pursueth man. Gregg escorted them to the front door and said goodbye as if they had been welcome guests. Only after he had watched them until halfway up the path and then shut the door did he allow his anger and fear to surface. How could they be so bloody silly; being that bloody silly, how was he ever going to persuade them of the truth?

*   *   *

As Park accelerated away from the pavement, Noyes, who had chosen to be a passenger, said: 'It's a classic. Rich bitch of a wife treats poor husband with contempt. After a while, he starts dreaming of a life with her money, but without her; and having a considerable imagination, he works out how this could come about if only. After a while, he forgets the if only. It's just his bad luck that he'd no cause to know that every car in a fatal is examined by experts.'

Park drove very carefuly around the right-hand hairpin, noting as he did so that workmen were replacing the damaged section of Armco barrier. 'I just still can't see him doing it.'

'In this day and age, a saint will sup with the devil if the price is right. And is he so spotlessly noble as he'd love us to think? He married her

184

for her money.'

'We can't be sure of that.'

'When he was declaiming his innocence a moment ago, did he once tell us he couldn't have killed her because he loved her?'

'His kind don't say that sort of thing.'

'How the hell would you know? Take off those bloody rose-tinted spectacles.'

Park braked to a halt at the T-junction. He accepted that his respect for certain qualities was hopelessly and snobbishly out of date, that the moral climate of the country had changed completely, yet he still believed that there were those who lived by old-fashioned standards . . . The road was clear and he drew out.

'All we need to complete the picture,' Noyes said, 'is to find he has a little bit of fluff tucked away who's already deciding how she'll redecorate Ankover Lodge.'

*　　*　　*

'The meat wants another thirty-five minutes and there are potatoes roasting,' Mrs Mabey said. 'I've put the pinger on. The peas need to be put in boiling water. Can you remember that?'

'I think so,' Gregg assured her.

'Are you sure you don't want me to come in over the weekend to do your grub?'

'That's very kind of you, but no thanks. I may go out for a meal one day or both.'

'It would do you a power of good to get away from here.'

She left. He went through to the larder and poured himself a Cinzano and soda, drank it quickly, poured himself another. The detectives had taught him something. Innocence was a defence only when one was clearly not guilty. How could he make them believe him? They'd even silently called him a liar when he'd denied knowing how much Diana had been worth. It was virtually impossible to prove a negative. Because he'd been brought up to observe another person's privacy in all circumstances and Diana had never volunteered the information, he had never tried to find out the details of her financial affairs. There was a wall safe in their bedroom in which were a few things of his—passport, for instance—and her jewellery and papers. Not once had he looked through the quarterly statements from her stockbroker or her accountant's figures. Yet he felt certain that if he'd explained this more fully to the detective inspector, he would have just met more poorly concealed contempt for his stupidity in thinking he could be believed . . .

It occurred to him for the first time that now he would have to read through all those papers. And the greater the capital, the stronger motive the police would believe him to have had.

He went upstairs to their bedroom and

186

opened the built-in cupboard in which hung her many dresses and at the back of which was the wall safe. Lingering in the cupboard was the scent of the perfume she had worn. He suffered a sense of loss so overwhelming that he turned away and stumbled out of the bedroom, his sight blurred by tears.

CHAPTER TWENTY

Park replaced the receiver, stared down at his desk. According to Fixley, senior partner in Trumbell & Co., some six weeks before her death, Mrs Gregg had consulted him. Under her existing will, her husband was the sole beneficiary. If she drew up a new one, would she have to leave him a proportion of her estate; if she didn't and should she predecease him, would he be able to claim through the courts a part of it? She had taken the matter no further before her death.

Park had no doubt how Noyes would receive this information. Faced with losing the luxurious lifestyle to which he'd happily become accustomed, Gregg had decided to murder his wife ... And yet, no matter how the evidence mounted, Park could not believe that even when faced by a financial cut-out, Gregg would murder first the dog and then his wife. Which, Noyes would say, merely confirmed that he was far from sharp-witted.

*   *   *

Thanks to a cross-boundary agreement between the eight divisions of the county force, Menzies was free to drive into Shinstone to talk to the employees of Abbotts Gallery once he'd advised someone in A Division of his intention to do so.

He entered the narrow, long, ground-floor showroom. A woman—no beauty—of about his own age was seated behind a small desk, talking over the telephone; she smiled a welcome. He looked about himself. A number of paintings hung on the walls; paintings left him cold. Pieces of furniture were carefully set out and one, a very heavily inlaid writing desk, was spotlighted; far too fussy. To the right of the assistant was a small, elegant dressing table, behind which were a pair of gilded girandoles; on the dressing table was a teddy bear. He walked across to examine the bear. Its smile suggested it had just finished a couple of pounds of honey. His young nephew, at the stage of teddy bears, had a birthday coming up . . .

'He's a good example.'

He turned to see the assistant had replaced the receiver. 'I reckon it would do my nephew a treat.'

'It is a Steiff.'

188

'Does that mean something?'

'One thousand five hundred pounds.'

'Are you blagging me?'

'I don't understand.'

'This really costs fifteen hundred quid?'

'That's the asking price, yes.'

'When it's missing a bit of fur behind the ear?'

'Adds authenticity.' She smiled briefly. 'The thing is, Steiff are probably the most famous of the makers. You can identify their work by the button in the ear.'

'Who'd credit it? Fifteen hundred for a teddy! So my nephew's going to have to make do with Homer.' He stepped up to the desk. 'My name's Detective Constable Jim Menzies.'

'Oh! . . . You're here because of what happened?'

He nodded.

'It's awful!'

'Isn't it?' he agreed. 'Are you the boss?'

'Me? I'm just the secretary, receptionist, duster, and assistant mover.'

'Then I hope they pay you four wages. Is the boss around for me to ask a few questions?'

'Hang on and I'll find out.' She used the internal phone to speak briefly. 'If you like to go upstairs, you'll see Laura's office to the right.'

He crossed to the stairs and climbed these to reach a second room of similar form and dimensions. There were more paintings on the walls and more pieces of furniture which even to his philistine eyes were of a lesser quality than those below, several show cabinets in which were figurines, and a couple of small statues, one of which surprised him because it didn't need a mind as active as his to decide the couple were not playing postman's knock. The office was a glassed-in area, crammed with desk, files, a large bookcase, and piles of magazines on the floor. Behind the desk sat a middle-aged woman with sharp features, very carefully groomed and dressed. She reminded him of his English teacher of several years ago. He introduced himself and explained the reason for his visit was that the crash in which Mrs Gregg had died had been engineered . . .

'You're saying it wasn't an accident?'

Even the way she briskly cut her words short was reminiscent of the English mistress. He wondered what her opinion was of split infinitives. 'The way the brake lines were weakened, it was inevitable they'd fail under heavy braking.'

'My God!'

He listened with impatience as she expressed her fears of a society that was proving ever more violent; finally, he interrupted her. 'What I'm after is any help you can give us in identifying who could have sabotaged the brake lines. Obviously you won't know directly, but you could maybe tell us something which will give a lead since you must have seen a lot of the Greggs.'

'She was here frequently, of course. But perhaps not as much as she might have been.'

'What makes you say that?'

'If she'd given more time to the business, she'd have made it even more successful.' She hesitated, then said: 'I've been wondering. What will happen to the gallery now?'

'It depends who inherits it.'

'That'll surely be Mr Gregg?'

'I've no idea, but that's what one would expect; provided, of course, things were smooth between them.' He saw her expression tighten and judged there was something to be learned. Gregg's wife, with a woman's need for sympathy, had confided her suspicions that her husband was having it off on the side? 'Naturally, there'll have been problems, won't there?'

'Why should there have been?'

'She was rich, he was ... Well, from all accounts, the money he made from his books wouldn't impress a dustman.'

She spoke angrily. 'You think success in art can only be measured in terms of money? History is filled with the names of truly great artists who were poor throughout their lives.'

'Sure. But however good his books, if he's not making much out of them, things must at times have become a bit rough between him and his missus.'

'Why?'

191

His English teacher had had the annoying habit of cutting the ground from under comfortable assumptions with a challenging 'Why?' 'Usually things don't work out if the wife's so much richer than the husband.'

'Because of pride? Mr Gregg does not suffer from false pride.'

'You obviously know him well.'

'I've met him only occasionally, but I've read all his books.'

'And that tells you what kind of a man he is?'

'Of course.'

'So what kind is he?'

'Warm and friendly, talented, but too responsive to other's opinions. An artist needs to be something of an egoist in order to keep confidence in himself. Sadly, Mrs Gregg did not help him do that.'

'You're saying she was always on at him?'

'She did not understand him.'

'It's usually the husband who says that.'

'In what way?'

He didn't try to explain his weak joke. 'It must have been tough for him at times. In that sort of situation, a man often looks for some kind of consolation. Other company, for instance.'

'What are you suggesting? I wish you'd speak more clearly.'

'Sorry, but I had a useless English teacher at school ... What I mean is, a husband looks around for someone who'll be more sympathetic and bolster his ego. Maybe it was like that for him?'

'I have no idea. Nor can I see it's any of your concern.'

'But it could be. There's no knowing what's going to turn out to be important. Let's just suppose Mr Gregg found a sympathetic friend. Now that obviously could be a very significant fact.'

'Are you trying to suggest that he could have had a relationship with another woman and that that might have something to do with his wife's death?'

'It's one of the possibilities we have to consider.'

'How ridiculous!'

'Our job is . . .'

'In your job, you should be able to understand people. Mr Gregg isn't like his wife; he'd never, ever think of betraying his marriage.'

'But she would?'

She looked away, her mouth tight, very annoyed with herself for having spoken so impulsively.

'Has she had an affair with someone?'

She did not answer.

'You must tell me.'

'I know nothing.'

'You like Mr Gregg, don't you?'

'Not in the sense you probably mean.'

'All I mean is, you've liked him when you've

met him because he's sympathetic and you think his writing's great. Right? Now when we start trying to find out who was responsible for Mrs Gregg's crash, we have to ask ourselves who might want her dead and, as always, the husband has to be high on the list. So if we learn he has a girlfriend, things can begin to look a bit black for him . . . But if it's her who's been playing around, it's obviously different.' He hoped that she would not immediately realise that the motive might change in form, but not in degree. He waited; silence could sometimes be so much more effective than words.

She went to speak, didn't; she fidgeted with a button on her dress; she looked at him quickly, then away. She sat very upright as she said: 'A man came into the gallery and said he wanted to speak to Mrs Gregg. He was very well-spoken and I thought he was probably someone who needed to sell something from the family collection because of taxes. I told him she was out. He asked me to ask her to ring him and gave me a telephone number. Naturally, I asked him his name—he just said John. When she returned that afternoon, I told her what had happened and she was obviously very disturbed. There was a lot of work which needed doing and she had said she'd spend the rest of the day with me doing it when she got back, but she left, becoming very annoyed when I tried to remind her.

194

'I forgot the incident until a few weeks later when there was a telephone call and I recognised the voice. Mrs Gregg was here and she took the call after sending me out of the office to do something which she must have known didn't need doing. When I returned, she told me she was going up to a two-day country house sale near Birmingham which she'd previously decided wouldn't be worth the journey. On the second day, there was a very important call from Amsterdam which needed a quick decision that she would have to make. She hadn't told me where she was staying and had left her mobile because she said it wasn't working, so I contacted a dealer I knew would be there and asked him to get in touch with her. He said she wasn't at the sale that day and hadn't been on the previous one.

'Just before she returned, I happened to come across her mobile and I tried it before taking it to the shop for repairs—it seemed to be working perfectly. When she arrived, I told her that and then said how I'd tried to get in touch with her. She accused me of spying on her. She became so objectionable that in the end I gave in my notice, even though I so needed this job as after my husband died . . .' She drifted into silence.

'But you didn't leave, so what happened?'

'The next day, when I was beginning to clear out my things, she arrived and immediately apologised and told me I musn't leave; her mother had been very ill and that's why she hadn't gone to the sale and why she'd been so upset. She took me to Rigorso for lunch to make amends.'

'That was saying sorry in a very big way!'

'Which is part of the reason why I . . . Well, didn't believe her—she was never more generous than she felt she had to be. She could have guessed that a straight apology would have been enough since I so needed the job. Naturally, I accepted the apology, telling myself that it was none of my business how she behaved or if she was deceiving her husband . . . It's wonderful how flexible a conscience can become,' she said bitterly.

How long ago was it when the man came into here?'

'A little before Christmas.'

'Have you heard or seen anything more of him?'

'He's rung once or twice when I've answered; more times when she's answered and I've been pretty certain it was him.'

'When was the last time?'

'The middle of this month.'

'What happened afterwards?'

'She didn't come in for a bit; when she did, she said her mother had been ill again.'

'You only know the man as John?'

'Yes.'

'And there's nothing more you can tell me about him?'

196

'Only the telephone number he gave me.'

'You can remember that? You must be in the genius class!'

'It was a local number and I have a friend in America whose zip code is the same. I wish . . .' She stopped.

He was unconcerned about her wishes. 'What is the number?'

CHAPTER TWENTY-ONE

The elaborate garden surrounding the eleven-storey building was well tended; there was a porter, in smart uniform, behind the curved reception desk. 'Your names?' he asked, his tone distinctly offhand.

'County CID,' Noyes answered sharply.

The porter's supercilious manner changed. 'One moment, please, while I speak to Mr Anderson's staff.' He spoke over the internal phone. 'Will you go straight up. It's on the eleventh floor.'

Noyes and Park crossed to the nearer lift which quickly and silently took them up to the top floor. They stepped out into a foyer that was carpeted wall to wall and furnished with four hunting prints and a Waterford vase, filled with cut flowers, on a small, elegantly inlaid side-table. As they approached the only door, made of some richly dark wood that gleamed in the electric light, it was opened. A small man, dressed in white coat, black tie, and striped trousers, said: 'Please come in, gentlemen. And may I have your names?'

Anderson was tall, ruggedly handsome, and possessed of that air of condescending pleasantness that came from an inner belief of superiority.

'Detective Inspector Noyes and Detective Sergeant Park, sir.'

'Good morning, gentlemen. May I offer you something to drink?'

'No, thanks,' Noyes replied.

Anderson turned. 'That'll be all, Stevens.'

Stevens left, closing the door quietly behind himself.

'Shall we sit?'

More command than courtesy, Noyes thought, having to work hard to suppress his dislike of the smooth arrogance.

Anderson sat back in one of the leather-covered armchairs. 'Satisfy my curiosity and tell me what brings you here.'

'We're investigating the death of Mrs Gregg, who was killed in a car crash in Addington a fortnight ago. You may have read about it?' He paused; Anderson made no comment. 'The car was examined by the police to try to determine the cause of the crash; it was found that the brake lines had been tampered with so that the brakes would fail under heavy pressure.'

'You are saying this was a case of murder?'

198

'Either that or manslaughter.'

'The world has become a dangerous place.'

'You don't seem disturbed by the news.'

'Would you expect me to be?'

'Yes. Since you knew Mrs Gregg.'

'I don't remembering saying so.'

'Did you know her?'

'As a matter of fact, yes, I did. And, contrary to your inept observation, when I read in the paper of her death I was greatly saddened. It is not, however, my habit to wear my heart on my sleeve.'

If he did so, Noyes observed, there'd be plenty of room left. 'When did you first meet her?'

'Several years ago.'

'How many?'

'Perhaps ten. It was before I was married, of course.'

'Are you suggesting you didn't see her after that?'

'I see no reason to suggest anything.'

'I have reason to believe you made contact with her before Christmas, last year.'

'Then surely it would be more logical for you to state your reason rather than ask a question to which you believe you know the answer?'

And up yours! 'You went to Abbotts Gallery to speak to Mrs Gregg. When told she was not there, you left your telephone number so that she could ring you later.'

199

'Really?'

'Did you call at the gallery?'

'And if I deny that I did?'

'I will be forced to ask the manageress to identify you.'

'I see.'

'You admit it was you?'

'An admission implies at least a hint of guilt. I will agree that it was I.'

'Were you having an affair with Mrs Gregg?'

'When we first met, we became close friends.'

'I'm referring to the past year.'

'There can be no valid reason to answer.'

'I'm conducting an investigation into a very serious crime and your evidence could be of vital significance.'

'Really,' Anderson drawled, for the second time.

'Do you want to become publicly involved, suffering all the attendant publicity?'

'A threat?'

'A question.'

Anderson stood, crossed to the far wall and pressed a bell push, returned to his seat. The door opened and Stevens stepped just inside the room. 'Yes, sir?'

'A Scotch, please.'

'Very good, sir.' He left.

'Prior to your visit to the gallery, when had you last met Mrs Gregg?' Noyes asked.

Anderson thought about the question for

quite a while before he answered it. 'My marriage was not a success—is any? After my wife and I parted, I decided to sell the estate because there seemed little point in continuing to suffer severe financial penalties merely to preserve the past; governments laud preservation, then impose taxes that make this impossible. Since I would no longer be living in a very big house, it seemed sensible to sell much of the contents. The quality of many pieces ensured there would be great interest in the sale and Mrs Gregg attended this in her professional capacity. We happened to meet by a portrait of my great-great-grandfather; a publicly respected man whose private life was, according to family legend, charmingly immoral.'

Stevens entered with a glass of whisky and soda on a silver salver. He presented this to Anderson, left.

Anderson drank. '"I often wonder what the vintner buys..." A puzzle I feel sure would test even your powers, Inspector.'

Noyes, certain Anderson was amused because he didn't know what that was all about, sought a way of puncturing the other's self-esteem. 'And having met Mrs Gregg again, you set out to renew the close friendship?'

'Life is seldom that simple.'

'Then what happened?'

'At the sale, we had very little time to talk since on my part I was leaving to go to London, and on hers, there was one particular piece of furniture she particularly sought which was about to be auctioned.'

'However little, it was obviously long enough for you to find out about the gallery.'

'She happened to mention that she owned it.'

'So you got in touch with her?'

'Your conclusion is again incorrect. At the time, it was not my intention to see her again; old flames seldom burn as brightly as new ones. But circumstances changed and after a while I decided to move out of London and find a *pied-à-terre* in England and somewhere in the South of France—well away from the stamping grounds of the lager louts, of course. I mentioned my plans to a friend in property development and he recommended this flat. I found it adequate so bought it. It was only after I had moved in that it occurred to me to make contact with Mrs Gregg.'

'Why didn't you get in touch with her at her home?'

'I had no idea where she lived.'

'It would have been easy to find out.'

'Perhaps. But you should know as well as I that husbands can be very territorial and resent their wives' past friendships. I left Mrs Gregg to decide whether her husband and I should meet.'

'That you did not was entirely her decision?'

'Indeed.'

'Did you see her often?'

'From time to time; when it suited us both to do so.'

'Where?'

'Here and there.'

'Were you screwing her?'

'Are you trying to be crudely objectionable?'

'Adultery is an objectionable habit.'

'A moralist as well as a detective?'

'Did she ever suggest she was afraid that her husband suspected she was having an affair?'

'She once described her husband as so naïvely trusting that even if he found her *in flagrante delicto*, he'd accept her denial that he'd been cuckolded.'

'When was the last time you saw her?'

'I suppose it was roughly the middle of last month.'

'Can you say on what date?'

'No.'

Noyes stood. 'Thanks for all your help,' he said, as sarcastically as he dared.

'I'm sure you'll be able to find your own way out,' was Anderson's rejoinder.

As the doors of the lift closed to cut them off from the foyer, Noyes said: 'Supercilious sod!' He pressed the button for the ground floor. 'But at least he's provided the last nail. Gregg decided to gain revenge as well as her fortune.'

'You're presuming Gregg knew about his wife. But Anderson was saying Gregg would never ever have allowed himself to believe his wife was two-timing him.'

'If Anderson told me duck, I'd stand tall.'

The lift reached the ground floor. They walked past the porter, who stared at them with open curiosity, and out into the sunshine, weak because there was high, thin cloud. As Noyes opened the nearside door of the car, he said: 'Don't ever again bang on about the merits of a gentleman.'

'That's one thing that bastard isn't,' Park replied.

CHAPTER TWENTY-TWO

Gregg's thoughts were interrupted by the front-door bell. He swore. For the first time since Diana's death, he had been able to concentrate his mind on work. He waited, hoping Mrs Mabey would be able to deal with the visitor, but there was a shout: 'You're wanted.'

He left the library and went along the corridor to the hall. Mrs Mabey said: 'I've put 'em in the green room.'

'Who are they?'

'The detectives,' she answered as if surprised he should need to ask.

In the green room, Noyes was standing by the window and Park was seated, his notebook open; Park came to his feet. Tension drove all thought of courtesy out of Gregg's mind. 'What do you want now?'

'Just the answers to one or two more questions,' Noyes answered.

'I've told you everything I can.'

'I doubt that.'

'You still don't believe me?'

'Why not sit down?'

Gregg was about to do so when he realised Noyes intended to remain standing in order to try to gain a psychological advantage. He ignored the suggestion. 'I do not know who tampered with the brakes of my car; I did not set out . . .'

'Do you know John Anderson?'

He had been so intent on what he was saying that for a moment he was bewildered by the question. 'Who?' he finally asked.

Noyes repeated the name.

'No, I don't.'

'Even if you haven't actually met him, surely the name is familiar?'

'It isn't.'

'He was a friend of your wife.'

'So he was a friend of hers. Why should that concern me now?'

'I'm sorry to have to say this, but Mr Anderson was a very close friend of your wife. He first met her about ten years ago . . .'

'Which is before I married. Why try to rake up something from the past? Do you get some perverted pleasure from that sort of thing? I'm sorry to spoil your pleasure, but I don't give a damn what happened before we were married.'

'Would you be concerned if a similar situation arose after your marriage?'

'It couldn't.'

'Why not?'

'Because we both held marriage to be a lifelong commitment.'

'Suppose you discovered, contrary to your belief, that that is not how your wife viewed marriage—what would your reaction be?'

'I never bother with hypothetical questions.'

'The close friendship between your wife and John Anderson was renewed towards the end of last year.'

Gregg suffered a wild anger that made him want to smash his fists into the face of the man who was slandering Diana. He forced himself to control his emotions.

'You either knew or suspected this.'

'I did not know, I did not suspect; since my wife never mentioned the name of Anderson, it's nonsense.'

'We have spoken to Mrs Rainer at Abbotts Gallery and she has told us that towards the end of last year, a man came into the gallery and asked to speak to Mrs Gregg. We identified that man as Mr Anderson and interviewed him. He admits that he saw your wife and their close friendship was renewed.'

'He's lying.'

206

'Why should he do that when the admission can only reflect badly on him?'

'Maybe he's so pathetic he can't get his kicks any other way.'

'He saw her frequently.'

'He never saw her.'

'The last time was probably around the middle of June.'

'The last time was many years ago.'

'You knew about this renewed friendship.'

'Since it didn't exist, that's an impossibility.'

'The facts say you did.'

'Then they're wrong.'

'The facts are that you and your wife hadn't been getting on at all well for quite some time. Then, to add to the problems, you learned that she was having an affair with a man she'd known before and who was very wealthy. You became convinced she intended to divorce you. Whilst you might then legally be able to claim a relatively small portion of her wealth, the humiliation involved in doing so was something you were not prepared to suffer. Yet without some of her money, your lifestyle had to drop like a stone. A small terraced house in a scruffy area is a very far cry from Ankover Lodge; beer doesn't taste so good when one's become accustomed to champagne. So you sought a way out of such a future.

'That was easy to identify. In her will, your wife left you her entire estate. But you knew she'd been in touch with her solicitor and guessed she was thinking of changing her will. So you worked out an ingenious plan which would enable you to kill her and escape all suspicion. Hopefully, the crash would be held to be an accident. But if it was not, the police would believe the murderer to be whoever had supposedly been threatening you . . .'

'Those threats were real. You've said other members of the jury would have also been threatened, so question them.'

'All eleven have been questioned twice; all eleven deny receiving any threats.'

'I told you Akers and Sharman voted not guilty. Make them admit what happened.'

'You're an intelligent man. Surely you can understand that there really is no point in going on and on denying the obvious?'

'I'll shout my innocence until I can find someone who'll listen and believe me.'

'Then I think you're going to become rather hoarse . . . You're only making things more difficult for yourself.'

'More difficult for you since you'll have to keep on working to find out who did sabotage the brakes.'

Noyes ostentatiously sighed. 'I suggest you do not consider travelling very far for the moment.'

'Are you arresting me?'

'No.'

'Then I'll travel where I want, when I want.'

They left.

Gregg slumped down in an armchair. Lying bastards. So certain he was guilty that in order to get him to confess, they were ready to use every underhand trick in their armoury. Diana unfaithful? Not in a hundred years. True, she and he had had their problems, but even if these had been very much more acute, she would never have dreamed of dishonouring their marriage . . .

For some reason, which he was only able bitterly to identify moments later, he thought of Joe. He remembered the first day he'd visited Diana's home and had been introduced. 'Isn't she the most wonderful, beautiful dog ever?' He'd naturally agreed—where new love was not blind, it had to seem to be. On a later visit, he'd asked her why she'd called a bitch by a male name? He'd been surprised by the sudden anger his question had provoked. 'It's short for Josephine,' she'd snapped and then sulked as he'd tried to apologise—without knowing quite for what. Now, the memory— forgotten for years—was so sharp that he seemed to discern a falsity in her anger, as if she had been using that to try to conceal another emotion . . .

Something was nudging his mind. An association in which Joe or Josephine figured. All he could immediately identify was the juvenile, 'Not tonight, Josephine.' Yet the fact of recalling one 'quotation' for some reason convinced him that the association of ideas was based on a quotation. He went along to the library and took down from the bookshelves the first of his five dictionaries of quotations. In the index, no Joe was listed, but Jo was. He turned to the page indicated. 'John Anderson my jo, John . . .'

Diana had told him that the dog had been given to her, but had never named the giver. John Anderson. He'd often wondered why her mother had been so hostile from their first meeting. Now, he knew. Her mother had been bitter because instead of marrying the wealthy John Anderson, she was going to marry an unsuccessful author . . . As marriage to him had become less and less emotionally satisfying, so the nature of her affection for Jo had become more and more saccharine; Jo was a substitute for John Anderson, who became ever more desirable in memory . . .

In recent months, she'd attended many more sales than in the past, yet unusually had bought little or nothing at most of them . . . Not long before she'd died, she'd stayed the night at her mother's because her mother was so ill—yet when he'd phoned, Susan Grantley had initially seemed not to know what he was talking about, then had quickly agreed that Diana had gone out to buy some medicine. Lying in the hopes that by doing so she might be helping to ensure there would be a Mrs Diana Anderson? . . . There'd been the night, after they'd dined with Vera and Jim, when to his surprise, her bitchy mood had suddenly become amorous and wanton: earlier she had returned home much sooner than she'd expected, so had she not met Anderson as arranged and had she tried to assuage her angry disappointment by awarding her husband what her lover should have enjoyed . . .?

*   *   *

The car turned into the courtyard and Noyes searched for a parking spot.

'Over there.' Park pointed.

Noyes drove across and carefully edged into the narrow space. He pulled on the handbrake, switched off the engine. 'Draw up a preliminary report, usual format. I'll get on to HQ and tell the super I'll be along to discuss whether it's time to send the papers on.'

'It is still virtually all circumstantial evidence and, well, if one gets things wrong at the beginning . . .'

'Are you accusing me of prejudging?'

'No, sir,' Park answered hurriedly, cravenly trying to head off Noyes's quick temper. 'It's just . . .'

'What?'

'I was wondering if we ought to question the two jurymen once more and see if a little pressure makes them change their stories.'

211

'What the hell makes you think it might?'

'I just can't see Gregg strangling that dog with a wire noose . . .'

'Consult an oculist,' Noyes snapped as he opened the door.

CHAPTER TWENTY-THREE

Mary Park had never been a slim beauty and an early onset of middle age, occasioned by three difficult births in quick succession, had not helped her appearance; but her serene, generous nature was so evident in her deep brown eyes that many considered her attractive. 'Don't you like the stew?'

'It's great,' Park, seated on the opposite side of the kitchen table, answered. 'You're a wonderful cook.'

'Too good, according to Chrissie.'

'Why's she talking so silly?'

'She thinks you've probably broken the fifteen-stone barrier.'

'Cheeky devil,' he said warmly. If he'd been asked to name the ideal life, his answer would have been the life he led (although more understanding seniors would have been a bonus).

'Jane heard the results of the mock exams this morning.'

'How did she do?'

'Not quite as well as she'd hoped. But as I told her, she expects too much.'

'She's ambitious.' He and Mary were so content with life that it surprised them their children could want more. Ambition was supposed to be a good thing, but experience had shown him that it had to be kept under strict control. Had Gregg really been unable to control his ambition . . .?

'You're off again,' she said. 'Staring at something a million miles away.' He speared a piece of meat with his fork.

'Is something wrong at work?'

'Not exactly. Only . . . Well, I can't help wondering if the DI's making a bad mistake.'

'That wouldn't be like him.'

'I know. But when someone disagrees with him who he reckons isn't very smart, he often can't take the time to listen.'

'Are you saying he won't listen to you?'

'Yeah.'

'Then he's not being smart. He ought to know by now that there are times when you can see further than him because you look at things from a different angle.'

'Maybe.'

'What's the problem?'

'Remember me telling you about the writer who was on a jury and said he was being threatened and then his wife died in a car crash because the brakes had been fixed? The DI's convinced he killed his wife and the story of the threats was all balls. Today we talked to a bloke who was having it off with the wife before she married and started up again in the last few months. The DI's saying that's the final proof Gregg fixed the brakes.'

'What about the rest of the evidence?'

'It all seems to fit. For Gregg's story to make sense, there'd have to be two other jury members who were nobbled, but we've questioned the two who voted not guilty and they both swear there wasn't any attempt to put pressure on 'em.'

'But you don't see things like the DI does?'

'It's the kind of bloke Gregg is. He's a . . . well, a gentleman. I said to the DI, Gregg couldn't kill a dog with a loop of wire, let alone murder his wife. He called me a bloody fool for thinking like a dinosaur.'

'Gentlemen have murdered in the past, surely?'

'Only because they weren't real gentlemen.'

'Isn't that a bit of a cop-out?'

'Maybe.' He mashed a piece of potato so that he could mop up the remaining gravy. 'Only . . . There can be people you'd stake your life on that they couldn't do anything to let themselves down.'

'Mr Noyes wouldn't, would he?'

'He'd find it easy to suspect a saint.'

'So what's going to happen?'

'He'll go to county with the report and he and the Super will decide whether the papers get forwarded.'

'What's your guess—will they be?'

'Like as not. If they are, there'll be shouts for some hard evidence and God knows where we're supposed to find that.'

'Then Gregg will likely be charged with murder?'

'Could be manslaughter, if it's decided that has a better chance of succeeding.'

'Whichever, you don't think it's right because he couldn't have been so brutal. So what are you going to do about it?'

'Me? There's nothing I can do . . . What's for pud?'

'Apple pie, if the kids have left any.'

'They'll hear from me if they didn't.'

'D'you want some ice cream with it?'

'So long as Chrissie doesn't start shouting that that'll add another stone.'

She put on the table a plate on which was a quarter of a home-made apple pie; from the small deep-freeze, she brought out a carton of vanilla ice cream. After pushing the pie and ice cream across for him to help himself, she sat. 'He must be going through hell.'

'Who?' he asked, as he emptied the carton.

'For Heaven's sake, Mr Gregg.'

'From the look of him, he is.'

'There's no way of proving he didn't do it?'

'Only if someone else on the jury admitted being threatened—I guess that would really tear a hole in the DI's theories.'

'Then talk to the two who voted not guilty and ask them what happened.'

'They've been questioned twice.'

'What's to stop you having another go?'

'The DI. I suggested that and he turned the idea right down.'

'Because he doesn't believe Gregg. But you've said you do.'

He was about to eat another piece of pie and ice cream; he held the spoon in front of his mouth for several seconds, then lowered it onto the plate. 'Here, you're not suggesting I should question 'em again?'

'Why not?'

'Because the DI would have my guts for garters for acting against his orders.'

'Then make certain he doesn't learn about it.'

'You think you can keep anything secret in our bunch? No way. I'm not committing job suicide.'

'Tom, love, think what things are like for Gregg if he's innocent—his wife's dead and you lot rush around in hobnail boots and tell him she's been unfaithful and therefore he murdered her. He must be out of his mind.'

'It's so bloody rough on him, I don't like thinking about it.'

'You've always told me that what makes your job so special is you can help people find justice.'

'I have to obey the rules.'

'You've bent 'em before now, when that was the only way of making certain things was right.'

'Only in very minor cases.'

'Then now's your chance to do that in a major one.'

He continued to argue, but he was on a losing wicket; not only had an innate stubbornness made him certain of Gregg's innocence, when he looked into her dark brown eyes he found he was ashamed of his reluctance to risk his own neck.

*   *   *

Park drove into Risham Green, a village that was not on a direct route from anywhere to anywhere and consisted of a pub and fourteen houses or bungalows set around a crossroads. Three Pines proved to be the misnamed—there were no pines—last bungalow on the edge of woods. He left the car, opened the wooden gate, walked up the gravel path to the front door, knocked.

The door was opened. Menzies had described Sharman as being so wet he'd be invisible in a swimming pool; for once, it seemed Menzies had not been exaggerating. 'Mr Sharman? I'm Detective Sergeant Park, local CID. I'd like a quick word, if that's all right.'

'I've said all there is to say.'

217

'Yes, I know, and I'm sorry to trouble you yet again, but there's something which has cropped up . . . Would it be all right if I came in?'

Sharman's face was a map of indecision. Park, smiling, stepped past him and into a space that was both passage and hall. Sharman hesitated, shut the front door. He said, staring down at the floor: 'We'd better go into the sitting room.'

The room was furnished with fussy precision and little taste. A couple of overlarge Abyssinian cats were settled on the chintz-covered settee and they stared at him with wary dislike. 'Lovely cats,' he said. 'My mother used to keep Siamese.' That was a lie, but he hoped it would sweeten the atmosphere. 'D'you mind if I sit?'

'Not on the settee.'

He settled on the nearer armchair and felt a spring twang. 'As you know, we're investigating the crash in which Mrs Gregg so tragically died and, as I'm sure Detective Constable Menzies told you, the brakes of the Ford were tampered with, which means someone deliberately intended to kill, or severely injure, whoever drove the car that day. What we have to establish for certain is who was the intended victim—was it Mrs Gregg or Mr Gregg? I'm sure you can help us with that.'

'I told the other detective who came here . . .'

'I know what you said each time, but I think you may have something to add . . . Or maybe even to change?'

'No.'

'Mr Sharman, whether or not you like it, your evidence is important since if you do not say what actually happened, you could be harming someone very seriously. I'm quite certain that's the last thing you'd want to do. Isn't that so?'

There was no answer.

'Mr Gregg was threatened over the telephone . . .'

Sharman said shrilly: 'No one threatened me.'

'Has it been explained to you that the moment the verdict was given, a threat could no longer have any effect so it became useless; then there'd be no point in carrying it out?'

'Then why was she murdered?'

'It's possible that there's no direct connection between Mrs Gregg's death and the trial.'

'Then why ask me about the trial?'

One of the cats stood, arched its back, yawned, then sank back and curled up.

'To prove a man's innocence. You wouldn't want an innocent man to suffer, would you?'

'Of course not.'

'Mr Gregg might well do so if you don't tell me exactly what happened.'

'Nothing happened.'

'Whoever tried to force him to obtain a false verdict would have known that however eloquent, on his own he would be most unlikely to be able to sway enough of the jury in the face of such strong evidence. So it's almost certain that two other members of the jury were also threatened to make them give false verdicts.'

'I wasn't.'

'Did you vote not guilty?'

'You've no right to ask.'

'I'm not allowed to question you about what went on in the jury room. But I've been told by someone else that you were one of two people who voted not guilty.'

Sharman began to pluck at the arms of the chair in which he was seated.

'The evidence against Lipman was strong because his victim was so believable and it's virtually impossible anyone could honestly have believed him not guilty.'

'I did.'

'How?'

'What . . . what d'you mean?'

'Did you imagine all the prosecution witnesses were lying? Did you think that if she had consented to sexual intercourse, she would then have accused him of rape, knowing the ordeal she'd have to suffer when she was cross-examined in court? You must have realised she had to be telling the truth.'

'Why won't you leave me alone?'

'Because an innocent man's freedom depends on you admitting what happened.'

'I wasn't threatened; I wasn't threatened.'

'The police will protect you from—'

'I tell you, I wasn't threatened,' Sharman shouted wildly. Beads of perspiration were forming on his forehead.

Park accepted that there was nothing more he could do or say that would make Sharman admit he was lying.

* * *

Park knocked on the front door of the red-brick house which was unmistakably Edwardian. The door was opened by Mrs Akers who told him that her husband had suffered a severe stroke and was in hospital, critically ill.

He returned to the car. He'd done his best. The knowledge that no one could do more than that did not make failure any the less bitter.

CHAPTER TWENTY-FOUR

It had taken time—a night of little sleep, a morning of tumbling thoughts, fears, and silent cries—for him to appreciate that having learned of Diana's affair, the police must now be certain he had murdered her. Yet he had not once suspected, far less known, that she was being unfaithful . . .

He was caught in a web of circumstances from which it seemed there could be no escape. His innocence mocked instead of defended him. Truth was what men thought it to be . . .

Again and again, the detectives had returned to the fact that if he had been threatened, so must two other members of the jury; he'd named Akers and Sharman as having voted not guilty which surely meant they had to be the two. Yet according to the police, each denied receiving any threats. Why? The answer was obvious. Even now, they were too scared to speak the truth. Akers, precise, pedantic, freeze-dried; realising that violence must shatter for all time the illusion that he lived in an ordered world, had been suborned by the threats; then had so hidden from his conscience what had happened that possibly he now believed he had not. Sharman, the perfect victim because he was the ultimate coward who could at the blink of an eyelid envisage agonies far more horryifying than any he was threatened with . . . To such a coward, the present future had always to be more terrifying than the future future. So what if he were threatened from a different quarter and most immediately? Gregg tried to banish the question, but it refused to go. If he continued to do nothing but wait for his innocence to save him, he would be charged with the murder or manslaughter of Diana and circumstances would falsely find him guilty. Justice, then, must surely give him the right to force the truth out of Sharman . . .?

He had always abhorred violence and believed it could never be justified except as the last defence. Was he not trying to defend himself? Yes, but Sharman was offering him no violence. Was that true? There was mental as well as physical violence and who could deny that deliberately to allow an innocent person to be found guilty was mental violence . . .?

For the first time, he could appreciate to the full the truth in the saying, principles and life make uncomfortable bedfellows.

*　　　*　　　*

Sharman, a bowl of cat food in one hand, opened the front door. Initially, he stared blankly at Gregg, then fear flooded in. 'What d'you want?' he asked shrilly.

'To hear the truth.'

He went to shut the door, Gregg used his shoulders to force it fully open; he teetered backwards, spilling much of the cat food on to the floor as he struggled to keep his balance. 'You can't come in,' he blubbered.

Gregg shut the door. To the right was an opened door. 'In there!'

223

Moaning, Sharman scuttled into the sitting room, carelessly brushing aside a cat as he went; the cat fled. Gregg followed him. He cowered against a chair.

'Tell me the truth and you'll end the day as healthy as you started it ... You were threatened to make you give a verdict of not guilty, weren't you?'

He shook his head.

'Weren't you?' Gregg's voice rose. 'And after I'd reported being threatened, you received a second one?'

'No!' he shrieked.

'And you won't admit it because you're terrified that if you do, the threat will be carried out. I've news for you. The threats you received will be child's play compared to what I'm going to do to you if you're stupid enough to go on lying. I'm about to be charged with the murder of my wife and only your evidence will convince the police they're wrong. Since I've nothing to lose and everything to gain, I don't give a shit how much you suffer so we'll start by putting your nuts in a vice and tightening it fraction by fraction, as an hors d'oeuvre.'

Sharman's terror overwhelmed him and he lost control of his bladder.

Gregg stared at the snivelling, terrified man and experienced bitter disgust—disgust at himself, not Sharman.

They heard the front door open. A woman

called out: 'Roland. It's me.'

The sitting room door was opened and a woman looked in, clearly expecting merely to confirm there was no one inside. Because the door was only half open, initially she could only see Gregg. 'I'm very sorry . . .' she began, as she opened the door wider, then stopped abruptly as she caught sight of Sharman. 'My God! What's happening? What's going on?'

He rushed forward and clung to her. 'He's going to torture me,' he blubbered.

Bewilderment gave way to fear, but she faced Gregg. 'Who are you? What are you doing to my brother?'

Of medium height and slight build, she could offer little physical opposition, yet she was prepared to challenge him, no matter at what cost to herself, in order to protect her brother. Gregg said slowly: 'I came here believing I had the right to force your brother to tell the truth.'

'What d'you mean?'

'The truth that would prove I did not kill my wife. I've learned I have no such right and even if I had, I could not exercise it.' He took a step towards the door and she flinched and clasped Sharman more tightly to herself. 'You've nothing to fear from me,' Gregg said. 'I'm a burned-out case.'

He left and returned to his car. He felt as if he'd been wallowing in a cesspit.

Shirley Anstey often had to struggle not to regard her brother with contempt. At such times, she remembered their father, who had ignored his son, judging him to be a weakling; the headmaster of the prep school, who had been stupid enough to believe that an over-sensitive character was best hardened by being bullied; a shrew of a wife, who in two years had undermined the little self-respect her brother had managed to salvage from his youth . . .

As he entered the sitting room, she said: 'What have you done with your other pair of trousers?'

'Upstairs,' he mumbled.

'Get them and put them in the washing machine. Then they won't stain.'

He left. She stood, went through to the kitchen and opened the cupboard in which he kept the drinks. He did not really enjoy alcohol and there was only a bottle of sherry. She didn't particularly like sherry, but she poured herself a full glassful. She felt much as she had the moment the policeman had told her her husband had had a serious accident . . .

'Shirl, Shirl, where are you?'

'In the kitchen.'

He hurried in, came to a stop by the table and gripped that for support. 'Oh, Christ! He was going to torture me. It was ghastly. You can't think how ghastly.'

'Here, have a drink to help.' She filled a second glass and passed that to him.

His hand was shaking so much that he slopped sherry over the edge of the glass as he lifted it to his mouth.

'Let's move into the other room and then you can explain what it's really all about.'

'Nothing,' he mumbled.

'Some performance for nothing! What truth was he trying to make you tell? How can anything you say help him prove he didn't kill his wife?'

'I don't know.'

'He certainly thought you do. Is it to do with the trial in which you were on the jury? But I thought that was a case of rape?'

'I tell you, I don't know what it's all about.'

'Let's go through.' She left the kitchen and went into the sitting room. She sat on one of the armchairs and a cat jumped onto her lap and began to purr even before she started to stroke it. She waited until he was seated, then said: 'What's his name?'

'Gregg.'

'Who is he?'

'Some kind of writer.'

'Did you meet him through the rape trial?'

'He was foreman of the jury.'

'So what happened here was to do with the trial?'

He said again that he'd no idea what Gregg had wanted, but she continued to question him

227

with quiet insistence and because he'd never been able to oppose her for long, eventually he admitted some of the facts.

'If you'll admit that you were threatened, that will somehow prove he didn't kill his wife?'

'That's what he kept saying. But I told him, I wasn't threatened. Only he wouldn't believe me.'

'In the circumstances, if you had been threatened, would you have told him so?'

'Of course I would.'

'You're certain?'

'I couldn't let him be falsely accused. My conscience would never let me be party to such an injustice.'

'You're lying,' she said sadly.

'I'm not. I swear I'm not.'

'Ever since you were young, you've become sanctimonious when you're lying . . . You were threatened, weren't you?'

He fidgeted with the glass, turning it around with his fingers. He suddenly said: 'Angeline's calling and I must go and see what's up.'

'It's Angeline on my lap . . . You're not going anywhere until you tell me the truth.'

There was a long silence.

'You and I,' she said softly, 'have never had secrets. Telling each other everything made it so much easier with Father. Please don't spoil what's so special between us.'

'I . . . I . . .'

'They threatened you?'

He hesitated for a long while, finally nodded.

'And you're still scared, which is why you won't tell anyone, even Mr Gregg, what really happened?'

He nodded again.

'Of course you're frightened—who wouldn't be? But you're going to have to tell the police.'

'No.'

'You must.'

'I won't.'

'They'll see no one harms you.'

'I won't. I won't. I won't.'

'But think what could happen to Mr Gregg.'

'I don't care.'

'He could be found guilty of something he didn't do because you won't save him.'

'I was joking. No one threatened me. D'you hear, no one threatened me.'

For once, not even the thought of what he had suffered in the past was sufficient to still the contempt she felt for him.

CHAPTER TWENTY-FIVE

Gregg was watching television when the phone rang. He picked up the cordless receiver, switched it on.

'It's Shirley Anstey.'

He searched his mind to identify the speaker and failed. 'I'm sorry to be so stupid, but do I know you?'

'Roland Sharman's sister.'

'Oh! ... I realise an apology doesn't even begin to make up for what happened, but I do apologise very sincerely. I can only offer the excuse that—'

She interrupted him. 'After you left, I asked my brother what was going on. He didn't want to tell me, but in the end I persuaded him to. He admitted that during the trial he was twice told to vote not guilty and threatened if he refused.'

'Thank God for that!'

'Will it help you?'

'It'll save me.'

'I'm afraid there is still a problem.'

'Which is?'

'As you must know, my brother is ... well, he's not a strong man. Yet his weakness sometimes gives him the strength of desperation. Although he's admitted the truth to me, he swears he'll never tell anyone else for fear that the threats are carried out on him.'

'The police will protect him.'

'As he kept saying to me, tragically the police did not protect your wife.'

'But if he won't tell them everything, I don't know where in the hell that leaves me ... I'm sure they'll be able to persuade him.'

'I'm afraid there's no guarantee. Partially

because you disturbed him so, now he's become totally terrified and maybe will never admit the truth again.'

'Are you willing to tell the police what he said to you?'

'Would I be ringing you now if I weren't?'

'Then that'll be good enough. I just wish I knew how to thank you sufficiently.'

'And I wish ... I wish I could be more certain I'm right to betray my brother.' She cut the connection.

* * *

'No,' said Sharman shrilly. He gripped the cat on his lap so tightly that it yowled, raked his hand with its claws, jumped down and raced under the settee.

'Your sister says ...' Noyes began.

'She's lying.'

'Why should she lie to us?'

'Because she's always hated me.'

Noyes had trouble in concealing his scorn. 'Far from hating you, she made it clear that her love for you is so strong it was only with the greatest reluctance that she got in touch with Mr Gregg.'

Sharman looked down at his hand. 'I'm bleeding! I've got to put something on or I'll get blood poisoning.' He stood and hurried out of the room.

Park said: 'Poisoning of any kind would be

bloody good riddance.'

'Belt up,' Noyes snapped.

They waited.

Sharman looked in through the doorway. 'There's nothing more so—'

'Come and sit down.' Noyes made it an order, not a suggestion.

Sharman sidled into the room and sat on the edge of the settee. The cat looked out, regarded him, retreated.

'Your evidence is vital to Mr Gregg.'

'It doesn't make any difference.'

'It does to him.'

'I wasn't threatened.'

'I've tried to explain that there is no danger to you . . .'

'His wife was killed.'

'The circumstances surrounding her death can have no direct connection with you.'

'Why not?'

'When the verdict was given, the judge was told ten members of the jury voted guilty, two, not guilty. That means two out of the three who received threats gave into them. No one's going to be after you when you were one of the two.'

'How can they know I wasn't the third one?'

Noyes's scorn finally surfaced. 'Do you really think anyone could believe you had that much courage?'

Sharman became very concerned with the large plaster he'd fixed to the side of his hand.

'Your evidence is vital.'

'I was never threatened.'

'You will not be required to give the evidence in open court. Your confirmation will probably mean that there can be no possibility that Mr Gregg might be charged with the death of his wife.'

'What happens if you find out who did kill her?'

'Your evidence will not be relevant.'

'But what if it is?'

'I've just assured you, it can't be.'

He took a deep breath. 'I was never threatened,' he said.

Noyes stood. 'You value your own skin far too highly,' he said, before he led the way out of the room, closely followed by Park.

Seated in the CID Rover, Noyes began to tap on the wheel with his fingers.

Park said: 'He needs a course of the treatment Gregg was going to give him, but didn't. Still, surely the sister's evidence is good enough?'

'Is it? In the face of all the other evidence? Suppose she's making up the story?'

'When it was obvious how much she hated having to tell us her brother's a lying creep?'

'She could be a damned good actress. She and Gregg could have been having it off and she's intending to join him in spending the inheritance.'

'You can see she's not that kind of person,'

Park protested.

'Not having a pair of rose-tinted magnifying spectacles, I can't.' Noyes started the engine, engaged first, drew away from the pavement. 'What's the score if we accept that she is telling the truth and her brother is lying?'

'The age of miracles isn't over.'

'There's no call for insolence.'

'No, sir.'

'Since Sharman, Akers, and Gregg were all threatened, it's virtually certain Gregg was the intended victim of the crash, not his wife. Someone's got to be really burned up to seek revenge by murder. Why?

'Go back in time. A rape case and the accused apparently just one more overeager Romeo. Question, who's going to go to all the bother, expense, and risk, of trying to turn the jury? Answer, someone to whom the rapist is very valuable only so long as he's free. How can that be? Because he worked for a security firm.'

'We've been down that road,' Park said. 'Pemberton's are small and never handle anything that would attract a heavy villain.'

'But when all the other facts can slot neatly together if that image is wrong, we can say it has to be wrong. So we'll go down that road again.'

*　　　*　　　*

234

Ryan spoke aggressively. 'I wasted a lot of time answering these selfsame questions last month.'

Noyes did not respond to the aggression. 'You know how our job goes,' he said pleasantly. 'We're either wasting our own time or someone else's.'

'That's fine when you get paid for doing it, I'm not. I've enough work for two, thanks to a couple off sick.'

'Then let's cut things short.'

Ryan's annoyance grew and his expression suggested he would have liked to don a superintendent's uniform once more.

'When did Lipman stop work?'

'At the beginning of June.'

'Then you kept him on until the trial started?'

'No reason not to. Rape doesn't stop a man being good at his job.'

'Have you handled anything since the beginning of June which would attract a really heavy mob?'

Ryan sighed. 'Didn't the DC who was here tell you? We're a small firm, always having to work bloody hard to keep our heads above water. If someone wants to guard a really valuable job, he goes to one of the big boys, thinking bigger means safer.'

'Which leaves room for someone smart enough to realise that therefore to think small could be to think safest.'

'There's always the chance; like there's always the chance of winning the lottery.'

'There's been nothing big on the horizon?'

'Haven't I said?'

'Then Lipman can't have known one was coming up. But that doesn't stop Mr Smart having discovered one would be and lining up Lipman in readiness to provide the essential last-minute details when these became known.'

Ryan linked his hands behind his head as he leaned back in the chair. 'I keep a close eye on employees' lifestyles. Lipman wasn't lighting fires with fivers.'

'Maybe he was being fed sweeteners only until the job was over so he didn't start spending.'

'They say everything's possible.'

'You can't help any further?'

'I've told you how things are.'

'You'll let us know if a big job does arrive on your desk?'

'I'll wrap the news around a box of Havanas.'

Noyes stood. 'Thanks for your help.'

'I'd say "you're welcome" if I meant it,' was Ryan's graceless rejoinder.

Park followed Noyes towards the door, then stopped and turned. 'There is just one more question.'

'The copper's mantra.'

'You've said your work's mainly local, but have you had a job from abroad since the beginning of June?'

Ryan unclasped his hands, sat up straighter. 'One.'

'Is that unusual?'

'Very, unless it comes through someone who's used us locally.'

'And this didn't reach you through any existing customer?'

'That's right.'

'When was this?'

'A fortnight ago.'

'What kind of job?'

'Provide two cars and six guards in smart uniforms to go along to the Chunnel to meet a train and escort a van that had come from Geneva through to London.'

'What was the cargo?'

'Wristwatches.'

'Rolex, Boucheron, that sort of class?'

'Not by an Irish mile. It was a new line in cheap but stylish analogues, aimed at knocking Swatch off their perch. The total wholesale value was down at only a hundred and fifty thousand.'

Noyes said, surprised: 'You had to provide two cars and six guards for a cargo worth peanuts?'

'It was all part of the campaign to launch the watches. We were being filmed collecting and escorting the van and the driver told me that there'd be an advertising campaign saying that every other watchmaker in the world had been so desperate to sneak a look at 'em that they'd had to be guarded every inch of the way.'

'Where did the van end up?'

'The Bank of England.'

'What?'

'They said it took 'em ages to get permission, even though they was just driving in and out—more advertising puff.'

'Did your blokes see the van leave?'

'No. Their job was finished as it drove inside the courtyard.'

'Who gave you the job?'

'The advertising company in London.'

'Their name?'

Ryan rested his elbows on the desk. 'Now you're beginning to tread very heavily on my business toes and . . .'

'You'd prefer to have my blokes under your feet all day trying to find out?'

Life in the force had taught Ryan to control his anger and unemotionally to judge the best course to take. He swivelled his chair round, pulled out the middle drawer of the nearer cabinet, searched for and found a particular file. He put the file down on the desk, opened it. 'Portesdown Advertising Agency.'

'Would you phone 'em for me?'

'So long as you pay for the call.' He dialled, waited. He dialled again. He called the exchange and asked them to connect him with the number. He replaced the receiver. 'The line's been disconnected.'

'Have you been paid for the job?'

'We never work to credit.'

'No trouble with the payments?'

'None.'

'Get on to Directory Inquiries and ask if they've a new number for the agency.'

Ryan's previous annoyance was gone— present an ex-policeman with a riddle and he becomes a policeman again. When the call was over, he said: 'They aren't listed.' He paused, then continued. 'There's a handbook which lists the names of most agencies; we ought to be able to get our hands on a copy without too much trouble.'

'My guess, only it's a little bit more than a guess, is that we won't find the agency listed anywhere because it was a temporary front for a government department. Since Gregg was the target for revenge, we know there had to be a really big job at stake that became busted because of him. The disappearance of the advertising agency tells me this was it.'

'I thought—' began Park.

'How many times do I have to tell you that a DS isn't paid to think,' snapped Noyes, well aware that Park had been about to point out the illogicality of what he had just said. They had come to Pemberton to find out if the firm had handled a large job since if so this would go most of the way to proving Sharman had been lying, his sister had been telling the truth, Gregg had not murdered his wife. Now he was accepting the last three propositions as fact in order to be able to assume the first was likewise. 'Pemberton was chosen because it's small and therefore inconspicuous; the van which came through from the Continent wasn't carrying a new line in watches, but something of very much greater worth.'

'Like what?'

'Could be many things, since the Government's involved. But remembering what's going on in the world and where the van ended its journey, maybe some of the gold that's being moved out of Switzerland because the gnomes have finally been shamed into disgorging war loot so it can be used to compensate a little for all the past horrors. Someone in Switzerland got wind of what was on the cards and set out to organise a heist. Information was the key to success, but Lipman raped a woman and was tried and found guilty, so he wasn't working for you when the final arrangements for meeting the van at Folkestone became known, which meant the job was off as it needed to be carried out with perfect timing if it was to succeed.'

They considered the possibility. It was Ryan who said: 'You could be right. But if you are, you're likely never to know for certain because no one's ever going to admit to the truth.'

'That's the story of our job.'

Ten minutes later, Noyes said to Park, as they drove away from the pavement: 'What made you think of asking him about a foreign job? Because Gregg said the second threatening phone call was made by a foreigner and you reckoned that therefore he couldn't be a gentleman?' He laughed.

*   *   *

Gregg left the Mercedes and walked through the small garden to the front door, rang the bell. The door was opened by Shirley Anstey. He said good morning and then, concerned by her expression, asked if he was interrupting something important.

She shook her head. 'It's just I was surprised to see you. I live on my own and only work part-time, so I'm in no rush.'

'I wanted to thank you personally for speaking to the police. It must have been difficult.'

'It was one of the most difficult things I have ever done. I've hated myself since.'

'Divided loyalties are a form of hell. But I hope it'll help a little to remember what you've saved me from.'

'In time, maybe ... I'm being very rude leaving you standing there—do come in.'

'Are you sure?'

'I wouldn't ask if I weren't.'

He stepped inside and she led the way into a sitting room furnished lightly and with cheerful colour. 'Would you like something to drink?'

she asked.

'No, thanks.'

They sat. He said: 'How is your brother?'

'Much as usual,' she answered bitterly. 'He ... You must understand that it's not his fault. When he was young ...' She became silent.

'My father used to say that if only we could escape being young, we might all be reasonable human beings.' Her head was slightly turned away from him, her gaze unfocused, and he could study her unobserved. He saw humour, compassion, courage, and strength. He hesitated, then said, more hurriedly than he'd intended: 'Would you be offended or upset if I asked you to have lunch with me somewhere here or in Shinstone?'

She turned to look straight at him. 'I'd be glad,' she answered in the straightforward manner which he had already come to expect.

*   *   *

Late September brought unseasonably fine weather so that autumn seemed to be on hold and winter well out of sight. Park walked into Noyes's office. 'Morning, guv. The crime reports.' He passed the single sheet of paper across the desk.

Noyes read, looked up. 'Isn't that the third incident in Marsham Road in the past few weeks?'

'The fourth, actually. Seems there's a family

moved in who are right tearaways; they've got the locals so scared that no one will agree to give evidence against them in court.'

'Then we're just going to have to find some way to change people's minds... Anything more?'

'Switzerland phoned through ten minutes ago.'

'They've finally woken up? Well?'

'They're sorry, they can't help. There's no record of any company which is supposed to have made the watches and shipped them to the UK and they can categorically deny there was any secret shipment of gold from any of the banks in the country.'

'Par for the course... So that's the end of the trail?'

'Seems so.'

'Shit!'

'But there is one other bit of news. It was Jim's birthday last night...'

'When I want social chat, I'll say.'

Park continued unabashed. 'He mortgaged half his year's pay to take his latest and dearest to The Carillon for dinner. Gregg was also eating there.'

'So? Now he can afford to eat there every day of the year if he wants.'

'The interesting thing is, he was with Sharman's sister and Jim says they looked interested in each other.'

Noyes's expression depicted a growing, yet

irresolute anger. 'Are you telling me that despite all his evidence seeming to slot in, we've been taken to the cleaners by a couple of amateurs?'

'I wouldn't think so.'

'Of course *you* bloody wouldn't.'

'Like as not, they didn't even meet before the day he went to the brother's place to try to force him into telling the truth.'

'The truth? What is the truth?'

It was odd, Park thought, how Noyes seemed unable to accept the obvious; perhaps this was one of the disadvantages of being intelligent.